CW00735574

Advance Praise

"Clonk! is a powerful detective story that leaps off the page. Rieger's prose is exciting and daring. *Clonk!* is a joy to read from beginning to end."

> — Mike Fiorito is an author and freelance journalist. His book *Falling from Trees* won the 2022 Independent Press Distinguished Book Award

"Deftly zigzagging among decades (1990s to 2020) non-chronologically, J. P. Rieger's *Clonk!* seamlessly interweaves the adventures and misadventures of a group of former Baltimore high school buddies — a diverse band-of-brothers outcasts — as they collide and intersect in adulthood with their most adjusted member, city-beat-cop-turned-detective Kev Dixit, who copes with an artful murder, deadly real estate fraud, and an ingenious arson for-insurance scheme. A wily witches' brew: witty, wise, and well-told throughout."

> — Michael Yockel, writer/editor and former *Baltimore City Paper* editor

"*Clonk!* is that rare thing: a funny novel that finds the perfect sweet spot between hard-boiled cynicism and hilarity. This delightful detective story seeks not only to decipher a crime, but also the enduring bonds of truly ridiculous friendships."

> — K.E. Flann, author of *How to Survive a Human Attack: A Guide for Werewolves, Mummies, Cyborgs, Ghosts, Nuclear Mutants, and Other Movie Monsters*, a NYT/Wirecutter pick for "Gifts We Want to Give"

"Familiar in a way that's sometimes affectionate and sometimes irritating, flawed, strangely reliable, clumsy, ordinary yet unique, unredeemable. These characters are all but abstract. Meeting them might feel confusing at first but it eventually turns into an understanding, an unexpected act of mutual recognition. It is very much like a high school reunion, happening many years later, marked by secrets, failures and an inscrutable sense of sympathy.

Clonk! brims with twists, time jumps and enigmatic appearances. It's because of that sense of closeness - and the fun that slips between the cracks - that we keep going back to its tangled storylines to make sense of an existing that, most of the time, is resolute in making no sense at all. As these characters seem to find out, that might very well be the best part of it."

> — Camilla Aisa, writer for *Record Collector* and *Shindig! Magazines*, U.K

"Gosh, I never realized Catholics could be funny, too. They are. This book is."

> — Bob Alper, Rabbi and Stand-Up Comic (Really) and author of *Thanks. I Needed That*

"In *Clonk!*, J.P. Rieger juggles multiple timelines to expose the shared experiences, the challenges, the wins and losses, and above all the humor that binds a group of friends together as they move through life."

> — Mike Stax, Editor, *Ugly Things* magazine

"*Clonk!* is a whimsical, nostalgic read spanning Baltimore's recent past, while keeping company with plenty of amusing scoundrels. Diner meets Tin Men."

> — Dan Fesperman, author of *Winter Work*

Clonk!

Clonk!

J. P. Rieger

Apprentice
House Press
Loyola University Maryland

First Edition

Library of Congress Control Number: 2022949959

Hardcover ISBN: 978-1-62720-459-0
Paperback ISBN: 978-1-62720-460-6
Ebook ISBN: 978-1-62720-461-3

Design by Erin Hurley
Editorial development by Erin Hurley
Promotional development by Rachel Brooks
Front cover illustration by Bondan P.S.

Published by Apprentice House Press

Apprentice
House Press
Loyola University Maryland

Loyola University Maryland
4501 N. Charles Street, Baltimore, MD 21210
410.617.5265
www.ApprenticeHouse.com
info@ApprenticeHouse.com

Also by J. P. Rieger

The Case Files of Roderick Misely, Consultant

To my Kristin—my Everything!

The stylist carefully placed the cape over the man who, minutes before, had been seated in the salon waiting room. Etta's eyes had followed the man and his stylist back to the salon chair. Men rarely booked appointments at the salon and she always wondered about these men. This one was not too bad looking and not too unmanly.

She was getting a little tired of sitting on the cramped seat. The crone sitting next to her kept invading Etta's space by flipping the page of her magazine onto Etta's lap. Etta innocently brushed the page and its weathered hand aside by fumbling for her purse tucked below the chair. She didn't need her purse but any physical movement would do.

The salon door opened and she glanced at the two pair of athletic shoes and skinny legged jeans entering—two young men. And then she looked up to see the ski masks.

Gillian, the receptionist, saw the handgun pointed at her face. "Bitch—empty out that cash drawer, now!"

She went immediately numb, too shocked to move.

The masked head moved in closer and this time barked loudly, "the fucking money, bitch… now!"

The man in the stylist's cape looked up to see the robbery in progress. Some of the patrons had begun to cry out in fright. He saw the receptionist fumbling in her cash drawer. He grasped both armrests, glanced up at the ceiling and braced himself. He stood up, pulled the cape aside and grabbed his wallet from his back pocket. He thrust the wallet open to reveal his ID and punched it into the air above his head.

"Police! Put the weapon down, immediately!" The voice bellowed throughout the salon. Every face instinctively turned towards the sound.

The man with the handgun looked over at the giant standing in front of the salon chair. He hesitated.

"I repeat—Police! Put that goddam gun down on the ground, now!"

The man's voice shook the glass windows in their frames. He again thrust his wallet into the air and began walking menacingly towards the reception desk.

The men in the ski masks looked from one to the other as the man with the cape moved towards them. The one without a gun said, "fuck this shit!" The two darted out of the salon door and jumped into the car idling outside.

Etta felt her heart pounding nearly out of her chest. The receptionist had almost collapsed but steadied herself with both hands on the reception counter. Slowly, everyone in the salon caught their collective breaths.

The man with the cape yelled, "quick—check the plate number!"

A couple of patrons got up and looked out the windows, but the car was turning rapidly into the road, kicking-up a fog of dust from the graveled parking lot.

The man quickly peered out the bay window near his salon chair. He saw the rear of the dark blue sedan charging away—with no plate.

And then, quietly, but growing in volume, he heard the applause coming from the reception area and the few salon chairs.

A woman yelled, "thank you Officer!" Others joined in with

their thanks and the applause grew loudly.

The caped man turned back from the bay window towards the group and said, matter of factly, "Oh, I'm not a police officer."

And before the confused faces could react, he drew himself up to full stature, swished the stylist's cape back with a flourish and bellowed, proudly: "I'm not a policeman. I'm an actor!" And then in a conversational tone explained, "that was just my wallet. I don't have a badge or gun or anything."

And then the lady who had been sitting next to Etta pointed toward the parking lot and said, "I think they've come back!"

They had. The dark blue sedan pulled back into the parking area and slid to a halt opposite the bay window. The man in the passenger side was already exiting his door as the car came to a halt. He calmly reached into the back seat, pulling out a sawed-off shotgun. He saw the policeman staring through the bay window and pulled off a first round. The shot blast crystalized the bay window and entered into the left thigh of the man. And before the caped man could shout, "get down!" the second shot blasted through the decimated window area, striking the man full bore in the chest and gut.

The gunman calmly re-entered the car, which drove away quietly.

As customers screamed and scrambled in panic, the caped man realized that he was lying on the floor of the salon. He tried to crawl to his feet but felt warmth flowing out from the cape. He collapsed again onto the floor and looked over to see tufts of someone's grey hair pooling with his blood on the salon floor. He thought it odd that this should be the last thing he would see on this earth. As he lay dying among the dust and hair, he closed his eyes and somehow felt a twinge of pride—his last, and certainly his finest—performance.

・・・

Six Weeks Earlier

"You are a mensch my friend, a mensch!"

Chris Waxley was wondering why in the hell the Troll had asked to meet up with him in a Starbucks—but, not just any Starbucks—one way the hell out on Pulaski Highway.

"Sure Brian, long time no see. What the hell's going on?"

They shook hands.

"Remember in the Godfather when what's his face says 'Someday I may need a favor?' Well, I need a little assist with something that is right up your alley, my friend, decidedly up your alley!"

"Okay—can I get a coffee?"

"Sure Amigo. Go for it. I don't drink that crap."

As Waxley waited on his coffee, he looked over at Golding seated about as far away from the counter as possible. When was the last time he had seen him—a funeral? The Troll had not changed much over the past ten or fifteen years. Maybe a little greyer in the hair, and even more overweight. As a fellow student at Ignatius, Golding always looked like a full-grown adult even as a teen. Mostly this was due to his being an Orthodox Jewish guy with yarmulke—and being short, overweight and assertive didn't detract from the perception.

Waxley returned to the table. Stirring his coffee, he noticed that there was not a single other customer in the Starbucks besides the two. "So, what's up?"

"Ok, you know I am not married, right?"

Chris didn't actually know but nodded.

"Here is my predicament. As a single, very eligible Jewish man who is not married yet at my age, you can imagine the pressures placed upon me to get hitched."

"Okay." Chris was not married, himself, but knew it had to be even worse for an Orthodox Jewish guy.

"So, my well-meaning parents have gone and hooked themselves up with a shadchan."

Chris looked on blankly.

"That is like a Jewish matchmaker. They find some eligible single woman and force her upon the innocent Jewish male. So, I am doomed as I do not in any universe see myself married to Ruthann Moskiewicz. I would truly rather be dead. The afterlife would be more entertaining and less stressful."

"So, this is like an arranged marriage?"

"No my friend. Such is not allowed in the Torah. But it is about the damned closest thing to an arranged marriage going!" The Troll shook his head in frustration.

"Do you have another woman in mind? You'd rather marry someone other than Ruth.... Marzipan?"

"Moskiewicz—but no. Well, yes! I would like to marry Katy Perry or some other hot vixen—you know, 'make Beyonce' my fiancé. Any hot, single, Jewish woman will do. I cannot be wed to Ruthann!"

Chris was thinking that Katy Perry and Beyonce' were probably already spoken for and not Jewish, but he let it pass.

"So where do I come in?"

"Ah, yes—it is time to strut your stuff on the runway, my friend! If my people see you and me together at the Caples' wedding next month, they will be led to believe that I, too, am gay! And, believing such, Ruthann and her family will run for the hills! I will be free!"

Seeing his friend's dumbfounded expression, the Troll added with vigor, "'Free at last, thank God free at last.' A little MLK at ya!"

Chris couldn't believe what he was hearing.

"Brian, there is only one problem. I am not gay!"

The Troll looked to the ceiling and laughed loudly. "Bullshit, my friend you are gayer than a two-dollar bill! Please give me a break!"

Chris was not sure about the relevance of a two-dollar bill and waited for the Troll to stop laughing.

"I'm serious, man. I am not gay! I like women!"

"Oh, please my friend, you are gayer than gay! You don't fuckin' walk, you sashay! Your wrist is in a constant state of limpness! Seriously, this is me, Amigo. 'The Troll,' you cannot bullshit me!"

Chris shook his head in disbelief—and shock. He was not gay and didn't believe that his mannerisms were other than those of a modern, educated, well-dressed and precisely manicured male.

"How can you think that? I'm telling you—I am a straight guy. No one has ever thought that I was gay!"

"Ha! You're killing me! C'mon, you were a male model. Everyone knows that!"

"What?"

"Your illustrious modeling career! I was in college. I read in the newsletter where you were doing modeling and you mentioned in the article that you were doing men's swimsuits and biking pants! Ha! Basically, you said that it was pictures of your ass dressed up in tight underpants and shit!"

Chris regrouped. "No. Well, yes, I did mention that the particular line that I was currently handling was men's sportswear and athletics but how does that make me gay?"

He admitted to himself that, pretty much, he wound-up being a butt model, but his modelling career was over and done, eons ago...

"Ok, how about you kissed a guy onstage—right, and don't bullshit me—it was that play you were in about the AIDS patients. 'Angels in the Outfield,' or some such shit?"

Chris was stunned again. Yes. He was an actor and actors had to follow scripts. Some scripts called for male-on-male intimacy. He couldn't believe that any of his Ignatius cafeteria gang friends would have even seen or heard of any of the plays he had been in. He liked doing cutting edge. He still did.

"You are thinking of 'Angels in America.' It won a Pulitzer..."

"Whatever. It's a gay story—and fucking sad as hell! I had to leave at intermission." The Troll was conscious of his slight fib. He left at intermission because he was bored and hungry.

"So, getting back to this—you want me to go to a wedding... as your date?"

"Well, no. We show up together and hang out—that's it, no funny stuff of course. My appearing with a... 'straight guy that others may immediately believe is gay'... Ha! Is all that I need. Will you do it, Amigo? Take one for the Troll?"

Waxley was still flabbergasted and with mouth opened, shook his head in confusion. Golding jumped in.

"Now listen, the Rabbi Joseph Telushkin once said, and I quote: 'the Gentiles feel bad about all the shit they've brought to bear upon the Jews and others, like through the Nazis and the Crusades and so forth and you can help a Gentile by letting him do you a favor. This will bring about a better understanding between our faiths... and possibly world peace...' So, how about it, isn't the Rabbi correct? Isn't helping me the Christian thing to do?"

The Troll had been trotting-out the Rabbi Joseph Telushkin since their Ignatius days.

"Seriously, is there really, actually a Rabbi Joseph Telushkin? Why would a Catholic guy care what a Rabbi would say, anyway?"

"Is there a Rabbi Joseph Telushkin? Jesus! He's the greatest we've had since Hillel! You know, Hillel once said, and I quote, 'If I am only out for myself, what the hell good is that? Do good and do it now!'"

"Ok, ok. Yes. I am an actor. No part exists in this universe that I cannot play! I will be your date at your wedding—as long as I am fed. Who's catering?"

"Yes! Amigo! We are back my friend! The dynamic duo! Should be Attman's."

"Good. I could eat corned beef... until it killed me!" Chris had lisped the line in his best Truman Capote and swept his arm across his brow, flamboyantly.

"Hell yeah—that's my boy! That's what I'm talkin' 'bout!!"

The Troll offered an enthusiastic high five to Chris, who responded back, cautiously, with a wet palm. The Troll wiped his hand on his pants leg. Chris took a sip of coffee. "By the way, I never asked you—how did a Jewish guy wind up at Ignatius? I mean, seriously?"

"Well, they didn't call it that back then, but I guess I was a 'diversity hire.'" Golding sucked back mucus from his sinuses, producing a horrifying, honking, phlegmatic sound. Chris was unfazed. The Troll had been doing that since high school.

"My parents were Old Pikesville and had no money. It was like a scholarship. You'll recall that my dad was—and is—a mortician. And back then he was an assistant. And, by the way, there is not a whole lot of money filtering down to the assistant's level. The deceased's family wants every last penny and you'd be surprised at how many families will stiff a funeral home. Oh yeah, we do all the shit work—and I mean it is shit work—and these assholes don't want to pay. They're 'too emotional right now to deal with such things,' etc. and there's not a fucking thing we can do. We can't unbury the dead. Being Jewish there's a lot more stuff—rules we have to honor that are second nature to us that you Gentiles don't have to worry about and would not understand, anyway."

Chris was thinking that digging up a body as a debt collection measure was probably not all that prevalent among Christian funeral homes, either.

"You were assisting your dad, right, but I heard you got into financial planning?"

"Oh, hell yeah, I had to break away from that shit. I've been counseling a few clients—select clients —with their investment portfolios. I've got a Maryland certification as a financial planner—it's like a license."

Troll was thinking that basically his two clients were his aunt and uncle, Frieda and Sid. But they liked his work.

"But to be up front with you, yes, I'm still a mortician and I still help my dad. I don't want to let him down, you know? And, yeah, I still got the hearse." He made a hitchhiking motion towards the parking lot behind him.

"Sure. I get it. By the way, why the hell did you want to meet here, way out in bumfuck? There's a really nice Starbucks near Old Court—that's near you, right?"

"Yeah—but this was safe. Anywhere closer may have had spies. There's nothing but hillbilly goyim out here."

They confirmed the date and time of the Caples' wedding, shook hands and went outside to the parking lot. The sun shone so brightly that they both squinted and shielded their eyes. Waxley threw on a pair of pseudo designer shades and sneezed, loudly.

"By the way, what's the problem with Ruthann?"

"Jesus? You haven't seen her. She's short, dumpy and way, way too fat... and feisty as hell! Forget it."

Golding looked over at Waxley's car. It was an ancient 2004, black, PT Cruiser convertible. The bumper sticker was courtesy of the SPCA. There was a basket of smiling kittens. It said "I love kitties!" Golding shook his head.

• • •

Dan Armbaugh was pissed. Lucky him. Today he got to "conference" with a member of the brilliant Baltimore City police force. Some smarmy sycophant was being delivered up to him by none other than his own boss and best friend, more or less, Todd Luchowski. Todd was Chief of Public Safety in the Governor's Administration. Armbaugh, Acting Chief of Security for the Maryland Aviation Administration, had to answer to Todd, officially. But unofficially, they were drinking and golfing buddies from way, way back. Mostly drinking. It pissed Dan that, A., he was being ordered—yes 'gently' ordered—around by his old bud; and B., rather than taking a direct swat at Armbaugh, Todd had passed the privilege onto a complete stranger in a different political food chain. Todd's brother, Michael, was married to the Deputy Police Commissioner. Oh well. Such was Maryland politics. And it pissed him off, royally.

He moved the two comfortable chairs that usually sat across from the desk over to the window, where he arranged them. He went into his coat closet and removed a slightly rusted, metal, unpadded, folding chair and set it up to face his desk. Why give anything away?

And it was not Dan's fault that the 'problem' had not been

solved. Homeland Security had punted the whole thing onto Maryland: "Jurisdictionally, the thefts took place beyond the clearance areas of our security designations." Yes, some asshole had found a way to get through Security and steal peoples' money and carry-on bags. Fourteen times in the last four months. And there was no arrest. Dan had done everything—thought of everything. Who the fuck was doing this?

He initially figured it had to be one of the employees of the now, countless 'retail unit' vendors at BWI. Some prick would wander around the waiting areas in the concourses and target the sleepy or inattentive or stupid. Who the hell would leave their carry-on exposed, post 9/11? So, the asshole would invariably 'pick' a few of the open or poorly attended purses or carry-ons, steal a few valuables or wallets and actually take one, two or even three carry-on bags.

Problem was, it was not going to be an employee of a unit because they'd have to wander off empty-handed during a break and suddenly return with one or more carry-ons. This would not go unnoticed. And there's really no good place to hide a bag at an airport. People take the warnings seriously. They alert Security to unattended bags. And the victims had flights all throughout the day—a guy on a break could not wander around all day and selectively hit targets.

It had to be a traveler—someone who got through Security, worked the gate area and took off for places unknown. He could simply remove the owners' tags, replace them with his own and check the extra bags at his gate.

And that's where things stood when Dan heard a light tap at his door. He wasn't sure what he was hearing. Usually, his Administrative Assistant would ring-in his appointments. But there was only that tapping at his door.

He opened the door to see a middle-aged, Indian-looking man in a crisp, navy blue sports coat and grey slacks.

"Can I help you?"

The foreign-looking man spoke: "Yes—are you Chief Armbaugh?" He smiled benignly.

"Yes—are you Todd's guy with the City Police?"

"I am!"

The Indian man held out his hand: "Kev Dixit—pleased to meet you." They shook hands.

Dan looked him over. 'Loser.'

Dixit took the metal seat without notice. "So, Chief Armbaugh, I've heard that you have been working this case, tirelessly!"

Armbaugh looked Dixit up and down. "Yes, it's been my focus for months. But I've virtually closed it. I've been pursuing some vital leads. Did you see my most recent report? Todd's seen it, I'm sure."

"Yes, I saw your report and was quite impressed. I am just a City cop. But it is very obvious that you have done everything possible and left no stone unturned. Impressive and fine work."

Dan was surprised. And suspicious. He didn't think the City cop would have an appreciation for his efforts.

"Thanks. As I said in the report, I believe the thief is a traveler. I ruled out employees spread throughout the airport because they wouldn't be able to take away the stolen carry-ons without someone noticing. And none of the stolen bags were ditched anywhere. My people have been all over it. And we've alerted the unit vendors to keep an eye out."

"Sounds rational."

"Yes. So, it has to be a person who travels a lot, picks a few pockets throughout the concourse, grabs a bag or two—or three—and gets onto a flight somewhere."

"Makes sense."

"So, on the days when the thefts occurred, I presumed that any flight departing that day could hold the thief. I requisitioned from every carrier, for every flight, each carrier's flight manifest. They were not easy to get. But the manifest gives us a list of every individual on the flight. The pilot, copilot, attendants, and every single passenger seated for the flight. There are hundreds of flights going out every day. I checked every one. I mean, every one. I looked for that one name—that one person who was flying out on the days when the thefts occurred. Flying anywhere. And... there was no person. Can you believe that? I mean, you'd figure—fourteen days with thefts over the last four months—there would have to be at least one name turning up as flying out of here on more than one of those days. And you know what? There wasn't. Unbelievable!"

Dan realized he was actually getting choked up. He was letting his emotions show, letting his guard down. He had to pull it together. This guy was a cop, not his confessor. The guy could not be trusted, no matter how damned pleasant he seemed to be.

Dixit sat back in the metal chair. It wobbled, almost fatally, and he quickly readjusted himself to avoid disaster. He shut his eyes and placed his fingertips together, under his chin.

An eternity seemed to pass. Dixit kept nodding, slowly rubbing his chin, still behind closed eyes.

Armbaugh watched intently.

Dixit was murmuring, "Yes, yes. You have been correct. Yes. That's it."

He sat upright in the metal chair, fighting against the chair's near collapse.

"The carriers—they let you down. They did not respond

adequately to your request."

"How's that?"

"You asked them to give you the names of everyone who had a ticket that day for the given flight. Am I right?"

"Yes. That's what I asked for."

"Ok—and they, dutifully, gave you the manifest—the list of everyone who flew on that given flight. But that's not what you asked for."

Dan was thinking that that it was, but he let it pass.

"You were not provided with the list of all the names you actually needed, despite your request. You have correctly reasoned about the traveler. And, I believe that you have, in fact, solved the case!"

Dan was more confused than ever but listened attentively.

"What I hear you saying—and correct me if I am mistaken— you realized that a ticket holder was your thief. You were looking for a traveler. So, the thief, as you correctly hypothesized, and will soon be identifying, did the following."

Armbaugh looked on, engrossed, but confused.

Dixit, again, closed his eyes.

"First, the traveler would find a flight that was likely to be over-booked. Look for Monday mornings—to places business-people travel, like... La Guardia, JFK or Newark. Or look for Friday afternoons—for business people departing BWI back to those places. Next, buy a ticket for a likely overbooked flight. Show up at the gate on the assigned date and in plenty of time and wait for a call for volunteers to give up their seats. Take the offer—preferably a cash bonus. Next, freely wander around the gate areas. Enjoy a sandwich. Have a coffee. You've got all day. Now, find and victimize your targets. Leave with your loot, at your convenience. Your name will not be on the manifest because you are not on the plane! You will, almost, be invisible."

Armbaugh snapped to attention and shook his head, vigorously. "Yes! That's it! The carriers didn't give me all the names! I had it, all along—dammit!"

"Yes, Chief. I understand that the administrative people for the airlines manage the manifests, which are held close to the vest. But ticketing is often out-sourced and handled by different people. One group may not talk to the other."

"Yes. That sounds right."

"So, when you identify and arrest your suspect and issue the final report to Todd Luchowski, just cc me, if you could, please. And, it will probably be a woman, because nine of the fourteen victims were females."

"Yes. You know, I didn't dare include that in my report—you know, 'sexism' and so forth!" Dan was improvising. He hadn't considered it.

"Yes, understood! So, I must say my goodbyes Chief Armbaugh and reiterate, again, what a pleasure it has been to meet you and see you in action, as it were!"

"Yes, thank you Officer. I honestly hope we have a chance to work together, again!"

The two shook hands warmly and Dixit made his exit, coming very close to providing a cinematic head nod and salaam to Armbaugh.

Dixit shook his head as he hustled down the hallway towards the exit. He was glad to get that performance out of the way. He had real work to do, on real problems. For some people, playing the humble, ethnic stereotype was expected and comforting. He had delivered his "Full Swami." It always seemed to work.

It seemed unbelievable to him that Armbaugh, in Aviation, had not considered the overbooking game. Plenty of cheap-ass fools with too much time on their hands worked the carriers for bonuses and penalties that way. This particular fool had simply taken the game too far and would soon be caught.

• • •

Twenty-five years earlier - February, 1995.

"What's this, up ahead. Why are they double-parked here like that? No hazards. It's dangerous."

"Yes, perhaps we should pull over and check it out."

Dixit didn't really want Officer Melody Jurgen, fresh from Harford County and transplanted to Baltimore, to pull over. This was the Block. No one cared about a double-parker on Gay Street. The car was a piece of crap—likely not stolen. But he had to make a pretense of following protocol.

Jurgen slid the City police cruiser alongside the car, craned her white, goose-like neck and peered over. She could see into the car, thanks to the mercury vapor street lamps.

"Is that guy dead?"

A man was slumped over his steering wheel. The motor was idling, gently.

Dixit sighed to himself. Looks like they'd have to actually get out of the car.

"Well, Officer, let's check it out. Pull in front over there."

The two disembarked. Jurgen grabbed her flashlight with her left hand while tightly clutching her holstered revolver in the other. She shone the light into the driver's side. The man in the car moved slightly.

"He's alive."

She tapped the flashlight tersely on the driver's side window. She tapped again, louder.

Finally, the man in the car, painfully, lifted his head from the steering wheel and groggily looked up into the blazing light.

"Sir, you can't stay double parked like this. Please show me your driver's license and registration."

The man clicked the window button, watched it roll down creakily and said, "Wha?"

Jurgen moved the light throughout the vehicle and saw something.

"Look Officer Dixit—there's a vial of some kind of powder sitting right there in plain view on the passenger's seat... and look—pills there, in the cup holder. Looks like yellow jackets!"

Dixit thought, 'great, now I'll never get home tonight.'

"We have to book this guy on suspicion of possession of CDS—those are Scheduled narcotics."

"Ok Officer. Let me take a look first."

And then he saw the face. He jostled Switzer by the shoulder.

"Hey Alan, it's me Kev. How are you?"

Switzer looked up, startled and confused.

"Kev? What the fuck are you doing way out here... in space?"

"Well, just making the rounds. Let me introduce you to one of our people. This is Officer Melody Jurgen. Officer Jurgen, this is Doctor Alan Switzer. He was Doctor of Pharmacological Studies at... where was it, Embrey-Riddle, in Florida?"

Dixit was hoping to make their interaction as 'Harford County' as possible.

Jurgen continued to shine the flashlight directly into Switzer's eyes.

"Sorry if I don't shake hands sir, due to communicable disease risks. What are those pills and what is that powder in that vial?"

Switzer looked around towards the cup holder.

Summoning his best demeaner he said, "those are my medications. I have a prescription."

"What about that powder?"

Switzer breathed in.

"Well, those are pharmaceuticals, too, under review by FDA. I am an authorized analyst."

Making that statement sapped almost all of his available energy and he slumped back onto the wheel.

Jurgen looked toward Dixit, confused.

"I've never heard of that Officer Dixit—is that for real?"

"Yes, Officer. I know this man. He is a medical doctor. I can say that, sometimes, he has an exhausting schedule, being a doctor and is often groggy. Don't let that concern you. He is a good guy—but obviously double-parked. That is wrong. I will write him up with an appropriate warning."

Jurgen drew back.

"Wait a minute. I'm not sure about this. I think those are narcotics. I think we have to impound the vehicle, take this guy in, run a narc scan and book him. Don't we have probable cause?"

"Understood, Officer. But, in the interest of efficiency, because I am your senior officer and can vouch for this individual, I am making the operational field decision that we write up a traffic warning, in this case—but, and this is important, we don't allow Dr. Switzer to drive the vehicle, due to his lack of sleep. I will drive the Doctor home in his vehicle."

Jurgen looked on, stunned.

"And, unfortunately, that means that you and I will have to split up for the rest of the shift. But, I have complete confidence that you can handle this on your own. Are you up for this, Officer? Am I asking too much of you?"

Jurgen looked positively aghast. But she steeled herself.

"Yes sir. I can handle it."

"Very good, Officer! I knew you could! Now, don't forget to

get the cruiser back to pool by 6 AM, sharp—they will hit us with a penalty if it gets in late."

"Yes sir! I have it."

Jurgen got the car back precisely at 5:59 AM.

At 6:01, she was at the Colonel's office, rapping gently on his door.

"I'm sorry to disturb you, sir. It's Officer Jurgen. Do you have a moment?"

Sansbury had just arrived and was very much in need of his first 'office' coffee of the day. He had already ingested three coffees at home. He saw it was a rookie—in Patrol, yet.

"What can I do for you, Officer?"

"Well, I don't feel one hundred percent comfortable with this sir. But they taught us in the Academy, that if any of our fellow officers, even a commanding officer, exhibited unusual or suspicious behavior or actions, we were honor bound to report such up the chain of command. And that's why I am here."

"Yes, certainly, Officer. Go on."

"Well, last evening, on second shift, my senior officer, Officer Dixit, who I otherwise respect and admire, greatly, did an odd thing. Rather than arrest a suspect for likely possession of narcotics and a related traffic offence, he elected to give the suspect a traffic warning and then proceeded to drive the suspect home in the suspect's car, which was technically, a crime scene, in and of itself. The whole thing was a little upsetting. I didn't understand why Officer Dixit would do this but I did not directly confront my senior Officer just as we were taught in the Academy."

Sansbury grumbled to himself. It was way, way too early for this shit.

"Yes, Officer. You were right to report this. The behavior was seemingly suspicious and not apparently representative of correct police procedures."

Jurgen exhaled.

"But, I have some important information for you. Prior to your arrival here, Officer Dixit communicated with me about this very situation. He explained his decision-making in a satisfactory manner. He also told me that he felt you were doing an outstanding job and that you should keep up the good work! So, I am completely satisfied in how you both handled yourselves last evening. Nice work!"

Jurgen looked both surprised, and downright pleased. A weight had been lifted from her shoulders.

"So, if there's nothing further Officer, I need to get back to work!" Sansbury smiled, charmingly.

"No sir. Thank you, sir!"

They shook hands briskly.

After Jurgen left, Sansbury sat down and moaned to himself. He was fed to the teeth with the lousy excuses for police that were dredged-up and spat out at him from every corner of the City. Of course, Dixit had not contacted him. But he trusted Dixit. That part was easy. Good cops did what they had to do. But what could he do with a rookie like Jurgen? This place would eat her alive.

• • •

March, 1996

Lou Ricciti and Pete Palanzo were stoked. The last few days had been a whirlwind. It took them all morning to clean up the conference room and clear the conference room table of files. But now they were sitting together at the table, looking out the window at Commerce Street, below. Blobs of soot-covered snow were still hiding under the buildings' shadows but would soon be gone. It had been the usual Baltimore winter—stretches of subfreezing temperatures, snow and ice, followed by recent, inexplicable days in the 40's and 50's. Finally, the shit would melt and be gone. And that meant Spring, and a more robust market, would follow. Not that things weren't pretty robust, just as they were.

Lou was still staring out the window, waiting for the new guys to arrive, thinking that it was hard to believe that he and Pete had built the fledging real estate and mortgage brokerage from scratch, just eight months before. They had made more money in the last six months than either, combined, had made, maybe, in the last six years. It was fucking nuts...

Lou had gone to the trouble of bringing a couple bottles of decent champagne, one of which was iced-down in the bucket on the window ledge, surrounded on the tray by champagne glasses. The other was waiting in the fridge in the office kitchen.

Pete got up and began to pace around.

"Man, I can't believe this happening! Scott came through for us, again, as always. What a prince!"

"Yeah—we are both fucking lucky dogs!"

Pete thought back to the meeting, and Scott's announcement, just five days ago.

● ● ●

"Vicki, Saundra, Lou and Pete! Jenny and I love you guys so much, but Jenny told me last week that we are expecting! So, it's time for us to make a move. We are finally going to get that family started! We are heading back to Jenny's in Albany. All of her people are there and she'll feel happiest being able to see her mom and dad, without having to hop a plane. Anyway, we all knew this day would come, but I am not leaving you in a lurch. I am bringing in some people that will help you grow the business in ways you never thought possible."

The group had looked on, stunned, but glad for Scott.

"Listen, these guys are pros. They will assist you in every way possible. I am staying on as a part time consultant. But, trust me—you won't need me. Okay, listen to this: Tex Heinlein and Martha Birckhead are loan people with a direct line to Chalk Investments. I know you've heard of Chalk. Yeah. That's the big fish we've been after. Chalk has a warehouse line and can fund anything and everything you can pull in. Jumbo, small—doesn't matter. Chalk sees a lot of promise in this market and Tex and Martha are the 'go to' people. They will basically be doing what I was doing in origination but at a much more advanced and lucrative, level."

Lou and Pete had found themselves nodding—wow, this was going to be great.

"There's another 'field' guy coming in who works with Tex and Martha. His name is Billy. I mean I haven't met him but he's part of the team. Like a guy in the trenches—can get stuff signed and shit."

They nodded some more.

"So, these guys will work with you to build this business! You guys are going to be so happy... and rich!"

• • •

Pete shook off his reverie when he heard Saundra announce on the phone intercom:

"Lou, Pete—they're here!"

They were expecting three, but a fourth person came into the conference room, too.

Lou and Pete introduced themselves and attempted warm handshakes all around. But the group seemed a little cold. And Lou was thinking that Martha had a bird's face. Seriously, he'd seen a lot better looking birds. And that 'Tex' guy was wearing a string tie and weird-assed looking rust colored suit with designer 'cowboy' boots. And he was no spring chicken.

The guy introduced as Billy Willoughby was a like an overly muscled fire hydrant. He had some kind of snake tattoo running along his neck. Just fucking weird looking. And who the hell was the fourth guy? The stumpy, bald guy in gray, polyester, three-piece suit? He didn't say.

They all sat and Lou got things started.

"Folks, I can't tell you how pleased I am to have you on our team! We've been making great strides in this market, thanks, mostly, to this man, my partner, Pete."

Lou gestured over to Pete, sitting next to him and began gently clapping, hoping to get everyone psyched. No one else joined in the applause.

"Anyway, I want you to know that Pete Palanzo is the originator and innovator of 'Market Forward Analysis.' Pete, take it away!"

Pete began to stand up to address the group, but instantly realized such was unnecessary and quickly sat back down.

"Thanks, Lou! Well, as a licensed appraiser, studying analytical statistics, too, mostly on my own, although admittedly, I did audit a few courses at Hopkins at night, I developed an appraisal system based on the "highest and best use" principles we appraisers are familiar with, and posited to myself... 'self, what if you were to base an appraisal on the overall potential of the real estate, as a going concern, in the future, post-closing?' I mean, to put it simply, doesn't it make sense that the true value of a property is not it's sales price, today, but it's sales price tomorrow? So that's the economic theory behind my 'Market Forward Analysis.' The reverse projection of tomorrow's value to the present is the most accurate valuation of the current market."

Lou, again, began to clap, but quickly stopped when he sensed he was alone in the effort.

Tex stretched his emaciated limbs out in his conference chair and placed his bony hands behind his head. "That's very nice Mr. Palumbo, sounds like a wonderful concept—and very flexible!"

The bird-like Martha nodded her head in agreement, looking like a chicken, pecking at corn. "It's Palanzo, Tex and thank you for that!"

Finally, the bald-headed man in the suit, who had never introduced himself, spoke: "I don't give a shit about that."

That was all he said. There was stunned silence.

Lou was thinking the voice carried a foreign accent. He'd heard that sound before in his old Little Italy neighborhood... the Polish guy who repaired shoes...

Pete was a little hurt. He was kind of proud of his work in the appraisal field.

Billy Willoughby chuckled to himself, got up and sat on the window ledge, next to the champagne. He began fiddling with the cork.

Lou tried to calm the waters caused by the bald guy's comment.

"Well, I agree. Ultimately, it's about performance in the marketplace. That's our strong suit. And that's why we are so eager to have you on our team. Scott said you would be great to work with. I know we are poised to dominate the Baltimore market. Baltimore has been and will be an incredibly profitable place for this company. Great days are on the horizon!"

But the cheerleading seemed to fall on deaf ears.

The bald man spoke, again, with that accent: "I believe you may be acting under some misimpressions. You speak of 'this company' and of us working together and so forth. This is our company, now. You work for us."

Willoughby was able to finally pop the cork. The sound startled Pete who almost jumped out of his seat. Willoughby chuckled louder.

Lou rallied.

"Look, sir—I don't think I caught your name? But why do you think you own this company?"

The bald man looked like he was suffering from a bout of gas. He winced. "Because I bought this company from your dear friend Scott Jansen. It's that simple. He owned 52 percent. I now own 52 percent. I also own a sizeable share in Chalk Investments. I am Otto Chalk."

Lou looked over to Pete as Pete looked over to Lou. What the hell was going on?

Martha spoke up. "Look it doesn't matter who owns the company, right? We all just want to make money." Her head bobbed again in a pecking motion.

"We help you, you help us. It's simple. Tex and I work directly with Mr. Otto Chalk. You two need to get your shit together and start producing loans and properties. And we mean a lot of them, quickly."

Pete spoke up. "We've been originating about twenty acquisitions a month."

Otto Chalk shook his head. "Deficient."

Willoughby laughed out loud. "I love the way he says that!" Tex joined in the laughter with Billy.

Willoughby was on his third pour of champagne; he hadn't offered champagne to anyone else.

Pete was beginning to feel nauseous. "What do you mean? How many do you have in mind?

Otto scowled. "We were led to believe that you two could produce about seventy or eighty a month. Twenty is for babies."

Willoughby laughed again. The laughter caused the snake tattoo on his neck to ripple and writhe.

Pete was feeling more nauseas and instinctively began looking around for a trashcan.

Lou was drowning, mentally, struggling to take it all in.

"Look, guys, we'll do the best we can but it's tough to get twenty good flips a month. We have to find and qualify people as borrowers. Pete has to do the appraisal paperwork."

Otto rolled his chair closer into the table and addressed Lou more intimately. "Ricciti, it's easy. HUD. They have the shit properties. Same everywhere. They are foreclosing and dumping shit on the marketplace all the time. Get their auction list. You will make fine borrowers both of you. Just change your names often and let the boy wonder produce the appraisals. Martha and Tex do the qualification paperwork. Chalk assigns at closing into the pool for the securities products that are packaged and sold. Everyone makes."

Lou and Pete looked stunned. Otto Chalk continued. "So, I am not coming back to this dirty place, again. Billy is staying here to make sure you stay on the job. That's our 'team.'"

Otto Chalk winced again and looked like a baby with bad gas.

The four of them got up. Lou and Pete stayed seated, still in a state of shock.

Tex giggled. "Don't you want to see us to the door? Manners?"

The two got up, clumsily.

Martha spoke: "We'll be here tomorrow. Get our offices ready. Oh, Billy doesn't need an office. He just goes where he goes, right Billy?"

Willoughby laughed again.

"Yep, that's me. A 'rovin' vagabond.'"

• • •

Karen Mortenson sat on the edge of her carefully made bed. This was going to be the saddest day of her life. She couldn't keep going on this way. Three—nearly four—years was a long time to wait for a partner to commit. Just too long. He'd be over soon and she would have to tell him. She began to cry, quietly.

He had said so many times—so often—how much he loved her. And all the nice things he did for her... he was always doing fun things for her. That's why she loved him. He was a good guy. That's why this was going to be so hard.

She had told him—warned him, he had to stop playing around with his future. He needed to get into a real profession. Being an actor was not a real job. Especially in Baltimore where actors seemingly worked for free—or nearly so. She was an actuary. She didn't find her job "fun" but it was why she could afford both of their rents. Jobs were never guaranteed to be "fun." Who thinks that? She shook her head in frustration and reached over to the nightstand for a tissue.

She stood up and tried to pull herself together. She went into the modern kitchen and poured a glass of tap water for herself. The sun was shining brightly through the windows, blazing off the polished surfaces of the kitchen décor.

Yes, he had proposed marriage a half dozen times. He truly loved her. She knew that. He told her he wanted a church wedding, too. They would work out the issues of his being technically a Catholic and she a Presbyterian. It would all be fine. Now she was smiling to herself, thinking of the wedding ceremony. But the feeling instantly turned to clenching sadness. She began to cry again.

She sat down on the Victorian love seat in her living room. This was not fair. Why in the world couldn't he see it? Him moving into that horrible apartment in Mount Vernon with some fellow actor roommate who moved out almost immediately once he got an offer in New York. And now she was paying the entire rent. It wasn't even safe over there. She couldn't stand being in that dingy, nasty place. That's why she always had him over to her apartment. They were lovers—but she didn't dare allow him to move in. Her parents would be crushed to think that their daughter was having sex while unmarried. She shook her head again in frustration.

Her mother would be sad—probably heartbroken—for her. But her father would be relieved. He just didn't like Chris. He wanted no parts of an actor. He had startled her, once, when he said that Chris seemed "effeminate." He was not. He was just charming, open and kind. And nice looking. She cried some more, frustrated. Chris' problem was that he lived in his own, ridiculous head. An unrealistic fantasy world. Couldn't he see that? She could never live in that place.

• • •

Three weeks later. April, 1996.

Lou hadn't been over to Little Italy for several weeks. He had always made it over, once, maybe twice a week to see his mom. But things had just been just a bit too busy. He barely had time to be around his own family. Things had gone very badly, very quickly. He would stop over his mom's after he met with Pete, whose house was caddy corner, across the alley. It was Pete's parents' home, but Pete was living with his mom again after his divorce. He had taken over the club basement.

Lou rapped on the back basement door. A sullen-looking Pete let him in.

"Seems like I haven't seen you for, gosh, almost a whole half hour."

"C'mon in."

Lou took a look around the club basement. He had seen it many times before when he was a kid. It was an awe-inspiring shrine to the Baltimore Colts. The cellar window curtains were white and blue. There was a wall of memorabilia including a framed, autographed jersey of Raymond Berry. A little lower was a framed black and white photo of Alan, "the Horse" Ameche, stumbling into the endzone to win the "Greatest Game Ever Played," so proclaimed the gold plaque below. A shelf held several footballs autographed by various Colts teams. A glass trophy box held a football signed by the team that won the "Greatest Game," the '58 NFL Championship. Johnny U's signature was prominently in front.

"Wow, this place is like a time capsule."

Pete looked around. "Yeah. My dad's stuff. He never wanted me to move any of it, so I respect his wishes and just leave it as it is. It's ok because it reminds me of him. And I'm just here, temporarily, anyway."

They both sat on the mildewed couch, covered by a stained Colts picnic blanket.

"Well, we're finally getting a new team."

"Yeah—bad deal for Cleveland. I didn't want us to steal a team just like that cocksucker Isray did to us!"

Lou was about to correct Pete that the name was "Ir-say" not "Is-ray," but he decided not to. He had only told Pete about ten dozen times before.

"Well, I think they have a name, finally. But I don't know what it is. I think 'Blue Crabs,' but I—we—have been too damn busy to know what's going on."

"Yeah, I don't know if I'm coming or going. Sleep is a luxury. This is a fuckin' hell..."

"Yeah—I'm worried."

They both sat some more.

Ricciti looked up towards the ceiling. "Had an idea—Blue Crabs could work. Think of like the crab holding out both claws, making like a "U" shape—like a horseshoe! Put that on the helmet like the Colts' horseshoe and watch fuckin' Irsay blow a gasket!"

"Yeah, the little shit would probably sue! That prick even took away our CFL Colts. May he die a miserable death and rot in hell!"

They sat quietly, some more.

Lou said: "Ok, we are in some serious trouble. We are not going to be able to get maybe more than 40 originations per month. And it's killing us and the girls just to get close to that. Saundra threatened to quit. Thank God she came to me and not either of those two pieces of shit. Those fuckers won't let us hire anyone. So, I honestly don't know what the fuck to do."

Lou buried his face in his hands, wearily, and then continued.

"It was almost funny that weird little Polish turd telling us to invent borrowers. We had been using legal, alternate surnames adopted for our investor clients and had it down to a science. But we were not the borrowers. The clients were. And they were glad to do it for the bonus. But we are never going to find enough investor clowns we can trust—no, wrong word—'depend on,' because you cannot 'trust' those assholes to do all this shit. I think we are going to have to be the fake borrowers. And that scares me."

"Me too. I know everything we've done so far has been above board. But if we turn that corner—go down that road... I don't know."

"And that asshole said to buy from HUD. Yeah, sure. That's just what you want. Let's register for the HUD auctions. Give them our full info. If anything goes south, they can trace us easily. Ridiculous."

• • •

"So, Chris is actually single? Pinch me!"

Gregory looked up from his dogeared script. "Well, yes but, no. He's not available."

"What does that mean, exactly—he found someone already?"

"No, it's not that."

"Don't tell me he's not 'out,' yet?"

Gregory folded the page over to save his place. "No, he's not 'out,' because he's never been 'in.' He's straight."

Roland was taken aback. "Seriously? You're delusional! He's queer, for sure!"

"No—well, we all thought so—everyone does at first, but all you have to do is talk to Chris for about five or ten minutes and you will realize he is straight. Very straight."

"That's crazy."

"Yeah—unfair, he's such a cutie—but he's like our little brother. We watch out for him. If every straight person out there were like Chris the world would be a beautiful place."

They were both now staring over at Chris who had seated himself on an aluminum chair in the opposite corner and going over his own script. Chris noticed them staring.

"What's up, guys?"

The two walked through the backstage area to join him.

"I'm Roland, Chris. I'm Fastrada. You're Lewis, right?"

"Yes. This is really wild. I love the script but the songs are a little challenging, though, aren't they?"

Gregory was thinking that the challenging part was having to hear Chris sing.

"Yes, this is more like the Fosse version—a lot of movement which I feel always makes singing a lot harder."

"Who did Zack decide is playing Pippin?"

Roland answered: "Marshall got it! The little bastard!"

Roland's shirt pocket began to ring, so he moved away to answer his cell phone.

Gregory spoke quietly to Chris: "So, I just want to reiterate that I am feeling for you, bro. Breakups are hard. She made a big mistake."

"Thanks, man. But you know—I don't blame her. She is a really, really good person. She just happened to have grown up in a very conventional environment. She just doesn't see much future for me or anyone in Baltimore as an actor. At least economically. I have to agree. It's murder getting a paying job. But—and here's the irony—just before she broke up with me, I told her that, in fact I had, just latched on to a pretty good, paying, acting job!"

"Really? Where?"

"I took a gig in 'Sim-Ex'—'simulation exercises.' Basically, they do a simulation of a particular kind of disaster or emergency and I play one of the people involved—usually a doctor, because the volunteers aren't as reliable in memorizing the medical jargon. That's why they need a few professionals involved."

"Really?"

"Yes, I know, it doesn't sound like much. But it does take acting skills and it does pay. In the big picture, I think it does some good, too. Local governments and private organizations need actors to play simulation roles realistically. Peoples' lives could be saved. And actors like me need the work. You get a decent paycheck, too, depending on the organization."

Gregory was thinking, 'and it's ok because you don't have to sing.'

"Well, I've never heard of that, but it sounds good—but it wasn't enough for your girl?"

"No. She said, 'don't they use mannequins for that sort of thing?'"

"Ouch."

"That's the thing. She's really a good person, but she just doesn't understand what we do. We change the world, a little at a time. We make people think and feel and laugh. What we do is important! It has a place in what we are as humans—it always has!"

Gregory began to tear-up and thought, 'that's my boy!'

Roland had concluded his call and was walking back towards Gregory and Chris. He was looking at the two, who, collectively, weighed less than Roland and was thinking, 'Shit—I will never be able to squeeze into those fucking tights. I will be a big, fat, gay laughing stock....'

• • •

June, 1993

"I didn't think so many of us would be here."

"Yeah, they say that the best turnout is for the tenth, twentieth and twenty-fifth — and then everyone starts dying-off! But this is not bad for the fifth."

Tim Whitson and Skip Weller clanked Coors Light beer cans together to toast.

"That's got to be Switzer, see—in the fatigues."

They were looking on from their spot in the shade by the Field House to the parking lot below. The man in camo fatigues was walking up the concrete stairs towards the Field House.

As the man approached, Weller put his beer can on the curb, clenched his hands together and delivered an ear-piercing whistle.

"Switzer—here!"

Clay Switzer waved and joined the two.

"Hey guys!"

The three exchanged handshakes and man hugs.

"Fuck, I could barely find a place to park down there. This is really a good crowd."

"Yeah—the 'five year' has really brought back a lot of us."

"I think it works because it's right back here at Ignatius and not some 'place' where you have to dress up and pay a lot."

"Yeah—a beer for a buck—works for me."

"And it's stag so—well, you know—it doesn't turn into a 'thing.' We can all just hang out and laugh that we no longer have to haul ass down to IPS in time or be locked out of the classroom by that crazy asshole Mr. Kavanaugh!"

The three laughed.

"And all the hot dogs you can eat, straight from the Alumni Committee grills which were last cleaned during the first Reagan administration."

The three laughed some more.

"Is that Dixit?"

They looked down into the parking lot to see a man in a Hawaiian Shirt ascending the concrete stairs.

"Hell yeah, look at that shirt—what a dick!"

Weller whistled again.

"Hey Dixit! C'mon—get the lead out—get up here!"

Dixit arrived smiling as he saw his old friends. He shook his head in admonishment.

"I can't believe you assholes made it."

"Well look at you—with that shirt you look just like fucking Don Ho! You are the fucking Hawaiian!"

Whitson said: "Who's Don Ho?"

Just then, Lou Ricciti and Pete Palanzo approached from the side.

"Whoa! The table is almost complete! Just need a few more!"

More handshakes and high fives were exchanged all around.

"Where's the Troll? I looked all around the lot for his hearse!"

"Dickhead, it's Saturday—that's their Sabbath!"

"Oh shit, yeah. I forgot."

Ricciti looked around some more. "Where's Waxley? Where's Linding and Reg?"

"Who the hell knows."

"Look, there's Linding. Holy shit—he's gained twenty or thirty pounds!"

Weller tried to whistle him over but Linding was engrossed in a conversation and wouldn't budge.

"Waxley said he couldn't make it. He's in a play tonight. We're both on America Online and when I asked him if he was coming, he sent back an email about the play. He said 'send my regrets and tell those assholes, howdy!'"

"Where's his play? Morris Mechanic? Maybe we should try to see it while its playing?"

"No, nothing that big. Some place called 'stop light' or 'spot light' or something. I'd never heard of it. Somewhere downtown—but not quite—almost downtown."

"He should have bailed and come out to this."

The group decided to move inside to the air-conditioned Field House and found a free couch. Dixit and Weller grabbed beers and moved a couple lounge chairs in.

"Not surprising about Waxley. Of course, he'd wind up an actor."

They all laughed knowing that the 'story'—one of the 'stories'—was about to be recounted.

Weller began: "So, I still piss myself to this day when I think about that time Waxley fooled those assholes on JV Football into the detention hall!"

They all laughed. The historic event was part of their collective DNA, now.

Ricciti took over: "Yeah those asshole sophomore jocks thought they were hot shit, throwing their gumballs and trash and soda cans at our table, laughing at the poor frosh!"

Palanzo jumped in: "And so Chris decides, 'fuck this—see you tomorrow boys' and the next day, just as those JV assholes start it up again, busting through the cafeteria door was the toughest, meanest looking priest you've ever seen in your life."

Palanzo began laughing and could not stop to complete the story.

Weller picked it up: "So, I mean, loud—he nearly broke the fuckin' door he opened it so hard. Every head turned to that door. In walks Father Waxley wearing the priest cassock costume from the Drama Club. He walks right over to those assholes at the JV table and tells them to 'stand up—get up, you're in detention, now!'"

More laughter.

"They shat themselves! Every one of them got up and marched out of the caf. down to detention with Waxley barking at them all the way telling them their asses would be cut from JV and maybe thrown out of school!"

"Oh my god, it was so funny! We followed behind pissing ourselves!"

More laughter from all.

Ricciti picked up the story as the others caught their breath.

"Then—you guys didn't all see it—you weren't there Dixit, right—you had class?"

"Yes, Advanced Latin—lucky me!"

"So, he corrals them into the detention room and tells them, 'you cannot leave detention hall for one hour. Take that time to think about what you have become: a bunch of little girls, throwing things! Think about acting like men for a change! This is Ignatius! It's not a goddam picnic or your kindergarten!'"

"So, we are almost all pissing ourselves. And we hide around the corner trying not to laugh."

Palanzo added: "I did piss myself. I literally did piss myself. It was so fucking hard to not laugh!"

"So, Waxley slams the door on them! He couldn't lock them in, 'cause he had no key, of course so he warns them again: 'Stay in there for one hour, until 3 PM—don't even think about moving out of there until 3!' And we all hang around the corner—by now, Waxley is pissing himself! So, about ten minutes later, we see the door slowly—ever so slowly—open. And the head of one of the biggest JV dicks starts to pop out to look around. Waxley rushes to the door and bellows—I mean screams: 'What the fuck are you doing boy! Get your sorry ass back in there or every one of you will be cut from the team and will be delivered over to your parents to explain why you are off the team and on probation!'"

The laughter rang throughout the Field House.

"And that fat shit jumped back inside that room so fast your head would spin! And Waxley slammed shut the door behind him so hard probably knocked him on his ass!"

More laughter rang out. Ricciti caught his breath and continued.

"And then we all just walked away trying desperately not to laugh! And those assholes never tried that again!"

By then, Linding had heard the laughter and elected to join his friends.

"Linding—remember the 42 bus and those assholes that used to egg us while we waited at our bus stop?"

And they all knew that an even better story was coming.

Linding began. "Oh yeah—you know those public school guys thought we were just a bunch of pussies going to a Catholic school. So, after they egged us from the 42 bus as it drove past us for—what was it—about five days in a row, we made a plan."

Ricciti continued: "Yeah, they thought they were hot shit and we knew that if they only saw a few of us, they wouldn't be able to resist getting off their bus to try to get us at close range. We knew they wanted to see us running away from them. So Waxley says, 'let me, Troll and Reg be the bait—you guys load up on eggs and hide behind the bushes—and a few guys take position farther down the street to get them when they're on the run.' So, of course, Waxley is standing out there in his usual weirdo clothes that make him look like a faggot, and there's Troll, the little fat boy with a beanie and Reg, of course—a skinny little Black dude—they look like perfect targets!"

Linding took back over: "And don't forget—except for me and Albright, no one else was bringing eggs and trying to fight back at that point—so they were not expecting anything."

Ricciti continued: "Yeah, so, sure enough—perfect timing— the 42 stops at the red light and those assholes see it's just Waxley, Troll and Reg. So, off they pour and begin pelting those guys with eggs, and then, all of a sudden we come roaring out and nail them—and I mean it was four or five of them and about ten of us and we creamed them—they were fuckin' covered with eggs — and running away like babies. Chris and Reg got their egg stashes from the bush and really nailed their asses, the Troll just rolled around on the ground, laughing."

The group was in hysterics and everyone in the Field House had gathered around to listen.

"So, they are scrambling, desperate to get their asses back to their bus at the next stop and, there you go—more of us come flying after them—and they get pelted some more!"

Linding picked it back up, because Ricciti could no longer speak. "And so Waxley and Reg are following them all the way to their bus yelling and chucking eggs—and the funniest part, the bus driver is like 'what the fuck?' Sees these egg-drenched assholes about to come onto his bus and tries to shut the door on them to keep them out, but they all squeeze back in except the last one kind of gets stuck in the door so Waxley literally kicks him in his ass and it pushes him through the door—and the door quickly closes and bus takes off!"

Linding was panting now. Ricciti took over. "It was the fucking funniest thing I've seen in my life! And they never tried that again!"

The entire room was swept into a bout of uncontrollable laughter.

• • •

Later, when the story telling was over, Dixit found Switzer. "So, how's the whole Switzer gang, been?"

"We've all been good. There's only two of my brothers still to get through college. Soon my parents will be free of us all!"

"That was the great thing about living down the street from you guys; if you wanted to get a game going, just knock on the door. Four of five kids would come rolling out, ready to play!"

"Yeah—we could almost field a baseball team!"

"What's Alan doing these days? Where did he wind-up practicing?"

"Well, he finished his residency at Glen Burnie Medical. They had him in the ER—he really loved it there. He said it was bat shit crazy, especially on the weekends. He has some great stories! But he had a few issues with some of the administration, there, so he wound-up in Perryton of all places I forget the name of the hospital... He has some kind of privileges there but started his own clinic just off of Main Street. I was kidding him, his patients can make it a trifecta—play pool in the pool hall on one side, get a tattoo from the parlor on the other side and then, if you get into a fight or get infected, he's right there for you in the middle!"

They both laughed.

"But he hates it out there and wants to get back to Baltimore. He will, eventually."

"So, you like being in the Air National Guard?"

"I love it! I love being around aircraft. It's not NASA, but it will get me up in space, eventually. Part of what I do goes into my certification for a pilot's license. That's the first step. It's just a matter of time."

• • •

May, 2010

Bhavna looked over at her husband with chagrin.

"We really have to visit this guy?"

"Well, we don't have to, but you could take a look at him? I spoke with him the other day, told him we should get together just to keep up and he put me off again. He's done that the last few times I phoned. Something doesn't seem right. He's hiding something—something he doesn't want us to see. Don't laugh, but I think he may be anorexic."

"An FBI agent—anorexic? Is that possible?"

"Well, you have to know the guy. He's a good guy. But something's off."

"Why anorexia?"

"Well, he was always a skinny kid—and man. So, I figured—I don't know...."

"Who's going to watch the kids?"

"We take them with us."

"Seriously? There will be a mutiny..."

"No, no. Vadin is 15 now. Old Alexandria is filled with young people. We'll drive around King Street, let him see the scene and cut him loose. He'll be ecstatic. He can phone us anytime. We can phone him. Beth, we'll keep with us, of course."

Bhavna shook her head and sighed. "A recipe for disaster."

"Well, it will be a short disaster. We'll be back home by dinner time. Speaking of dinner, we'll need something to bring for lunch. Can you make your famous chicken? When he inhales the aroma, he will have to let us in!"

"Great—more work..."

"But worth it!"

Kev gave her his most charming smile. Bhavna shook her head, capitulating.

Dixit was thinking about the last time he had phoned Reg. Reg had said that he still loved being in the FBI. He was assigned to Communication Technologies, exclusively. And they had set him up in his home. He never had to go to an office. It was perfect for him, he said.

• • •

Reg heard his doorbell ring. Sunday afternoon? Who the hell was that? He looked warily out from his condo peephole. Kev? And a woman and kid?

He yelled from inside: "Hey, is that you, Kev? What are you doing out there?"

Kev looked towards Bhavna.

"We thought we'd come by just for a quick visit to say 'hello,' since we were in the area."

Bhavna thought, 'why would we just happen to be in the area with homemade lunch for all? Come on Kev.'

The door did not open.

"Oh, guys, I am so sorry, but I am really, really jammed today. I've got a project due in hours and a big conference call to get on. I've got to take a rain check, I'm so sorry!"

He was waiting for them to sheepishly apologize and go away. They didn't.

"That's ok, Reg. Tell you what—you remember Bhavna, my wife, and daughter, Beth? Look, we wanted to bring in some lunch and just say hello—but I've got a more urgent problem. I have to go to the bathroom—quite bad! So, how about we just pop in, we drop off the lunch, I use your bathroom and then we get out of your hair?"

Kev looked over at Bhavna. Bhavna thought, 'it's a good thing he said he was the one who needed to use the bathroom.'

There was an almost endless pause.

Suddenly, they heard the sound of the latch chain pulled free and deadbolt slipped away. The door opened to a beaming Reg Marquis. He, waved his arm inside to invite them in.

"Welcome to my humble home, friends!"

He shook hands warmly with Kev and said to Bhavna, "you must be Bhavna! Kev has told me so many wonderful things about you!"

Of course, Kev hadn't actually. He gave Bhavna a respectful hug.

"And who may this be?"

Beth moved closer to her mother.

"This is our baby, Beth. Our son Vadin is out wandering around King Street, probably checking out the girls!"

Reg laughed. "Ah yes, to be young!" Kev looked around anxiously. "Back there Kev, sorry!"

Dixit made his way to the hallway to search-out the bathroom, but took a visual inventory along the way. He saw that a former bedroom had been transformed into a sea of cables, servers and computers. Otherwise, everything else looked pretty normal.

Bhavna handed Reg the chicken casserole, covered over with aluminum foil. The dish was exuding scents of cumin and coconut. Reg breathed in, deeply.

"Wow, this is going to be good! Should I just take some of this and that way you guys can have the rest later for yourselves?"

"Oh no, please Reg, we want you to have the whole thing. We can always pick up the dish, later."

Reg was doing a quick mental calculation, wondering about the feasibility of having the dish shipped back by UPS.

"Well, thanks—that is so generous, and believe me, I am going to enjoy it!"

He patted his average, but definitely present, gut.

Although not invited to do so, Bhavna and Beth sat themselves on the living room couch, as Reg took the casserole to the kitchen. She saw him pushing a few things out of the way in the refrigerator to make room for the casserole.

"Your condo is so nice, Reg."

Bhavna craned her neck and saw the glass patio door that led from the rear of the living area. The sun beamed beautifully through the glass.

She got up to take a look at the patio. The furnishings were still covered over, even though it was now May. He obviously hadn't taken advantage of his own patio and yard. Judging from the amount of bird droppings and dirt on the furniture covers, she doubted that he had used the patio at all, last year.

"So, Reg, what do you think of the Torpedo Factory? If I lived here, I'd visit there all the time."

"Yes. I hear it's a nice place!"

"Do you like art?"

"Of course, very much!"

Bhavna noticed that the walls held few pictures or art of any kind. She saw a photograph of Reg in cap and gown, smiling with his likely two parents. There was a framed "Tuskegee Airmen" poster on the opposite wall. There were no family pictures or portraits. It didn't look as though he had ever been married—and certainly, there were no kids.

"Reg, you know, this is the kind of neighborhood where you could get by without ever having a car. You could walk to almost everything you need."

"Yes—in fact, I don't own a car! Everything I need is right here!"

Just then, Kev came back down the hall. He was speaking on his cell phone.

"Ok—yes, right by the Banana Republic. See you in ten, big guy!"

"That was Vad—ready for extraction. He's going to ask you for forty bucks for a shirt. It's your turn to say no!" Kev chuckled.

Bhavna shook her head.

"Ok, let's leave Mr. Marquis to do his work, now!"

Beth hopped from the sofa and clung to her mother.

Warm goodbyes were wished all around, with promises that they would all get together again, soon. Once outside, they heard the sound of the chain latch and deadbolt being moved back into their places.

•••

Reg took a deep breath and sat on his living room sofa. It was ok, now. They were gone and he was safe again. He understood that Kev must have been concerned about him. Kev was the most faithful friend he ever had—and Kev barely knew him. And he barely knew Kev.

He put his hands on his face and began to weep. How the hell had it come to this? He figured that Kev would try to understand what was going on with him—and try to help him. They all, always, tried to help each other.

And then he thought back to his own pathetic efforts to help Ricciti and Palanzo. The U.S. Attorney, Wilhelm, didn't really care about Reg's contentions that the two didn't understand what they had gotten themselves into.

"I hear what you're saying Agent Marquis, but according to the statutes under which they were charged, the culpability of their mental state is not relevant. They committed the acts pro-scribed by statute. They're lucky that we let them plead-out. We dropped all the other stuff. They'll be fine. They'll get through this and have reasonably productive lives, although pleading to a felony charge has its consequences."

"But they won't be 'fine.' I mean, their families won't be fine. Look, Mr. Wilhelm, those two are obviously idiots. They were caught up in something they didn't really understand. If they take your deal, they will wind up in Jessup for, what, at least four years? Their wives and kids will suffer exponentially, relative to the white-collar stuff they got themselves into. I saw the file. You guys forfeited everything they had. I mean, that's restitution. Isn't that enough? They have nothing, now."

Wilhelm sighed. "Look Agent Marquis. This is not just about these two men. We are sending a message—a strong, but measured response. House flipping is a poison that ruins a community. Borrowers are victimized by unreasonable loans based on false, fraudulent appraisals. They can be subjected to crushing debt that will haunt them for a lifetime. The communities most exposed and victimized by this poison are populated by minorities."

Wilhelm peered at Reg over his tortoise shell glasses, for effect.

"And, lenders are ripped off, too. That means higher rates for all consumers. And the average 401 K owner—mom and pop—wind up with over-valued securities in their portfolios. They lose their retirements. We can't let this go unpunished. We're sending a message."

Reg crossed his arms and exhaled.

"And, by the way, we did cut them a break. We did not forfeit their homes. We could have."

Reg uncrossed his arms and looked to the ceiling and then back to Wilhelm.

"Their homes? Seriously? Their spouses had no idea what was going on. Palanzo was already divorced. He was living at his parents. Forfeit his parents' home?"

"Ok, but you see my point. The Office of United States Attorney has tried to be reasonable."

Reg sat back in the upholstered leather chair and re-crossed his arms. "Can I tell something about those guys?"

Wilhelm scowled. He knew he was going to hear it, one way or the other. "Sure."

"Ok. I went to high school with both of them. Ignatius. It's Catholic. My family lived on North Avenue, 1800 block. Yeah, I had a scholarship. I took the 22 bus cross-town to pick up the Ignatius school bus in the 'nice' neighborhood."

Wilhelm winced. He hated long stories.

"I was a scrawny kid. I was 5'7" and weighed, probably, ninety pounds. The 22 had a lot of mean, white, public school kids. The toughest ones sat in the very back of the bus. It was like a peanut gallery. They would harass and bully any kid they didn't know who seemed weak. That was me. I knew that if I wound up in the back, I'd be in trouble. But if I sat or stood near the bus driver, in the front, they couldn't harm me. So, that's what I always did. Or tried to."

Wilhelm looked at his watch.

"On this particular day, I got pushed in by the throng, almost all the way to the back of the bus. I had to take a seat next to some of the meanest kids on that bus. So, they immediately started in on me. There were four or five of them. Do you know the word 'splib?'

Wilhelm looked puzzled.

"No? Well, that's a word for a Black man. When a white kid calls you 'spliby' that is meant as an insult. That's what those boys began calling me, 'spliby.' And they were smacking the back of my head and neck and laughing and having a good old time. The biggest one stood up to get a good punch in and suddenly he hears a voice: 'get the fuck off that guy - now!' It was Ricciti. He and Palanzo rode the same 22 bus. They stood up and walked to the back. Palanzo—and you've seen him, he's a big guy—says 'what the fuck you assholes doing back here! Get the fuck off this guy or we will fuck you up, bad!' And that was that. Everyone sat back down and all was calm. Ricciti and Palanzo spoke their language—and spoke it for me. So, that's why I am hoping that you will cut those guys a break—let them have a better deal. Because they are basically good people."

Wilhelm hated to admit it to himself, but he understood. He was bullied as a kid, too. He did feel something.

"Marquis, I hear you. Ok, I'll take all this under advisement. I can't make any promises, though."

Once Agent Marquis left, Wilhelm thought about the case. He would have cut them a better deal, but their attorneys were crap. Their attorneys' ads and egos were as great as their skills were deficient. If he cut a break for those two, it would affect his cred in future cases. He liked having a leg up on the cast of criminal defense lawyers that crawled through their sewers to make his everyday life difficult. He sighed to himself. Cutting them a break would give their attorneys something to crow about. Something they hadn't earned. So, no breaks for those two.

● ● ●

Reg got up and went to his kitchen. He needed a drink, badly. He went into the refrigerator. He saw the casserole and for a split second wondered what it was, and then immediately remembered. He pushed it aside and found the metal can of Hawaiian Punch. He poured himself a tall glass. He knew it was mostly sugar, but he really liked it. He threw a couple ice cubes in and sat down at his kitchen table.

He drank some punch and sighed. Then he thought of Kev's visit. They probably figured he was agoraphobic. It wasn't really agoraphobia. He knew it was much worse than that. He was actually afraid of life.

• • •

Kev and Bhavna did not discuss their thoughts as they motored down 295 back to Baltimore. They didn't want the kids to hear anything that would frighten them or influence their views on Reg.

When they were finally alone, Kev spoke: "Ok, he's not anorexic. He's at a good weight. That's about the heaviest I've ever seen him."

"I agree. I saw he's got plenty of food in the fridge."

"So, what do you think?"

Bhavna shook her head. "You know I hate to do 'drive by' psychoanalysis."

"Yes, yes, but come on. Don't we still have 'Doctor-Patient Confidentiality' after all these years?" He smiled charmingly—or so he thought. "You can give me your thoughts, freely. You may share without concern." They had each declared this disclaimer countless times before.

She shook her head, in reluctance.

"Ok. Based on what I saw, Reg may be suffering from agoraphobia. He doesn't have a car. He hates opening the door, even to a friend. He has obviously never even walked around his own neighborhood. And he doesn't even go out onto his patio."

Kev shook his head, taking it in.

"Yes. I saw a bunch of empty cardboard boxes from Grainfields stored back at the end of the hallway. He's probably having his groceries delivered."

Bhavna sighed.

"And with agoraphobia comes depression. He is probably suffering greatly. The FBI is not doing him any favors. They found an agent willing to man their lighthouse for them, some kind of lonely, solitary job. I would guess that his position is feeding his agoraphobia. He'll need a lot of therapy, maybe drugs—and certainly a new job—to get free."

• • •

October, 1998

There it was on his appointment book. He had to take that damn test again. Dixit made his way over to the "Professional Development Center" to the "Training Lab." The "Training Lab" was, essentially, a small classroom filled with rows of tables holding uncomfortable plastic seats. He checked in with the proctor outside, turned in his cell phone, took a seat and unsealed the envelope. As in each of the other cases, the envelope held two sharpened pencils, a 'blue book,' and a one-page exam consisting of just three questions. He had thirty minutes.

He sighed to himself. He hated taking the 'idiot test.' Every officer had to take the test at least once per year. If you had put-in for a promotion, you could take it up four times per year. But there appeared to be no direct correlation between the 'idiot test' and promotions. And no officer every received a grade for the test. No one knew who 'graded' the exams. No one really knew why the exam was given. It was just a test.

He knew what lay ahead: One question would be 'touchy feely' about helping a challenged or disadvantaged person. One would be 'crisis management' about his reactions to a seemingly impossible situation. The other would be some sort of 'math' or 'logic' puzzle. He hated the logic puzzle the worst because he never seemed to 'get' what was being asked.

He had done six years in the street in Patrol, but he wanted to be a Detective in the CID. It bothered him to think that the idiot test could forestall or prevent his promotion. He felt that his responses to the questions in the past demonstrated his care, compassion and ability to act quickly in a crisis. Logic and math—he wasn't so sure about.

In past exams, he had always spent too much time on the other two questions, leaving too little time to work out the logic puzzle. Thirty minutes went by very quickly.

Feeling annoyed, he decided that, today, he just wouldn't give a shit. He was sick of the test and just wanted to get on with his day's work. The test didn't seem to make a difference in anything. He decided that he would make his responses to the questions just as stupid and ridiculous as the questions themselves. He pictured some intellectual type in horned rimmed glasses becoming increasingly puzzled and annoyed by his answers. That made him happy.

He read the first question: "As you entertain in your penthouse apartment, the lights suddenly dim. You feel engulfed in an eclipse-like darkness. Your guests become frightened and concerned. You hear an intermittent hissing sound—like steam forced out of a pipe. Your guests begin to leave your apartment for the elevator. What do you do?"

Dixit thought, 'Great, the crisis management question.' In the past he would have responded that the loss of power and sound of a possible gas leak meant that the building was in a distress situation; possibly even under a terror attack. He would have written that the guests must be prevented from using the elevator or engaging any electrical circuit that could potentially ignite the gas. The guests needed to calmly use the indicated stairways and move to the lobby and out of the building for safety. But he stopped himself and sat back in his plastic chair. He closed his eyes and felt an inspiration. He took a breath and wrote:

"I would tell my guests to not be concerned. Today was the hot air balloon race. A wayward balloon had gotten too close and bumped-up against the apartment building. The fabric of the balloon was parked against the outside windows of several apartments, blocking out the light, making the apartment dark. The sound they heard was the pilot igniting the gas jets to create more hot air in the balloon to get the balloon moving, again. There was nothing to fear."

He laughed to himself. 'That was fun.'

The next question read: "Little Johnny always stayed with his dad after school. Dad tended bar, but was proud that he could support his son. Johnny always sat at the end of the bar away from the other patrons and did his homework. But he was always happiest on days when a baseball game was playing on the big screen television. He loved to glance up from his work and watch the game from time to time. Johnny never had a chance to play baseball, because of his father's work schedule. But one day, he was in luck. His dad was able to take him to the park where other boys were playing. They let him in the game and he had a chance to hit. He chose a bat, took a practice swing and went to the plate. The pitcher threw and Johnny hit the ball with all his might! A base hit! Johnny dropped the bat and immediately began to run to first base, just like he had seen on TV. But all the boys began to laugh at him! He had run to third base, not first base, and was called 'out.' What should Johnny's dad do?"

Dixit shook his head. In the past he would have suggested that Dad comfort his son and continue to encourage sports. Dad should try to get Johnny into Little League or some other organized form of youth baseball. Or perhaps Johnny needed to be evaluated for dyslexia which might have caused his misdirection in running bases. But he threw all of that aside. He was on a roll now:

"Dad needs to sit Johnny at a table directly in front of the television screen when a game is playing. Obviously, Johnny was watching the game as reflected in the mirror behind the bar. All of the base runners would appear to Johnny to be moving in the reverse direction. Hence, Johnny thought that first base was to the left and ran to the wrong base."

He chuckled to himself. 'That was even better!'

He was ready for the math and logic question.

"Two trains are running today. Tracks A and B are parallel. One train runs from Duvall north to Centerville. The other train runs south from Centerville to Duvall. The northbound train departed on track A at 1 PM and ran at a speed of 40 km per hour. The southbound train departed on track A at 3 PM and ran at a speed of 70 mph. Mile and kilometer markers were placed along both tracks at appropriate unit intervals. At which mile marker and kilometer marker would the two trains pass each other?"

Dixit rubbed his eyes and read again. He slumped back in the plastic chair. This one was a ball-buster. He read the question for a third time and noticed something.

'A typo!'

Somehow, the southbound train was said to be running on track A, not track B! Track A already had the northbound train! He quickly wrote:

"Sadly, the trains never passed. They both ran on track A and collided. Emergency personnel were immediately called to the scene."

He laughed to himself. 'Done with ten minutes to spare!'

• • •

July, 1996

Billy Willoughby was smirking. "What's your problem Ra-Shitty?"

"Well for one, my name, as you know, is Ricciti, asshole, so I don't appreciate your trying to fuck with me."

Willoughby smirked again. "Ok. Mr. Ra-Cheaty! Is that better?"

"Cut the shit, pal. You're not being paid to fuck with us. Why don't you do your job and I'll do mine."

"I don't know what your problem is 'Shitty.' We got you two brand new photo copy machines and you're still producing less than forty a month. Seriously. That's a fuckin' joke. In Hoboken, they are clearing a hundred a month. I don't know what's wrong with you two clowns. Martha and Tex have been patient with you. I wouldn't be and I doubt Mr. Otto Chalk will be."

"Well, as you know we are working our asses off. We're not the only ones in this game, now. There's another guy working the West Side who owns a title company and has a direct line to all the slumlords unloading their shit. The guy is an asshole slumlord himself, so he can get a hell of a lot of properties, easily. Another shithead is the 'tax sale' king—and he's using all those properties."

"Not my problem."

"Well, you're supposed to be the man in the street, helping us get properties. And by the way, where the fuck is all the money we're supposed to be getting? We are getting less money, now, than before."

"Boo fuckin' hoo. Mr. Otto Chalk is not going to approve you assholes getting more until you turn this thing around for him. You eat what you kill. Nothing more."

• • •

Ricciti rapped on the back basement door. Palanzo stuck his head out, looked around to make sure the coast was clear, and let him in.

"Saundra gave her notice. I didn't dare tell that piece of shit Willoughby. I fear for her safety. I'll try to talk to Tex about it tomorrow."

"Tex, forget it—he's fucked up."

"Really, I should go to chicken-faced Martha? She's just as bad as Willoughby. Those two are psychos."

They were sitting on the mildewed sofa in the Palanzos' club basement.

"Willougby was giving me more shit today about our production. Saying that's why we aren't being paid. This is more fucked up than ever. That fuckin' Scott really screwed us. What a bullshitter. His phone line is disconnected. He's long gone."

"Yeah, what a turd he turned out to be."

Ricciti stared over that the Raymond Berry jersey.

"You know, we were happy, once. It's hard to believe that we transformed our transport company into a full fledge real estate company. But it makes sense—boxing up stuff to help people move, naturally got us into the real estate. That fuckin' Jansen had to come along and fuck us over."

Palanzo changed the topic. "Look, I want to tell you about something."

Ricciti looked like he didn't want to hear any more bad news. "Okay."

"This is weird but last week, Wednesday, I think, around 2 or 3, I needed to take a piss, so I am about to go into the men's room, when I stop because I hear Willoughby in there with Tex. So, I hear Tex laughing and then suddenly, I hear him fucking scream. I heard like a slapping sound—like a belt being struck or whipped around. And Tex is screaming and crying and begging Willoughby to stop it. I didn't go in, of course. I was fuckin' sick to my stomach and ran out of building down to Harbor Place to take a leak. I think those two are into something sick."

Ricciti shook his head. "Jesus. We didn't sign up for this shit."

• • •

February, 2002

"Did you see the guy in the hallway with our lost lamb?"

"Yes—please don't tell me he's representing the Respondent?"

Dr. Swenson looked to the ceiling, and with ennui, replied, "Apparently so."

The Maryland Board of Physicians was actively involved in Administrative Appeals and Hearings. Maintaining professional standards and protecting Maryland patients and patients' rights was its raison d'être. Flawed physicians were constantly before the Board, pleading their cases, looking for ways to claw their way back into that most sacred, ancient and learned profession.

Dr. Swenson was thinking, "Primum, non nocere." Swenson was a teaching Professor of Medicine. The Hippocratic Oath was driven into the brain of every first-year medical student. And yet so many could not avoid "doing harm, first." He shook his extremely bald head in disgust.

"I think we're being called in."

Doctor Gregg agreed. She had heard the gentle chiming sound, too.

The Administrative Law Judge read the prior decision of the Board and asked the Appellant for the grounds of his appeal. "If you feel that the Board committed reversible error in its decision of May 11, 2001, to permanently suspend the license of Dr. Alan Q. Switzer, please raise those grounds, now."

The strange man seen in the hallway stood.

"Your Honor, I'm counsel Rainwater Wells for the Appellant, Dr. Alan Q. Switzer." He glanced over to Switzer seated behind him and grasped Switzer's shoulder in solidarity.

Attorney Wells was wearing a baggy black, three-piece suit, shiny black boots and a turquoise stone string tie. Six feathers were attached to each breast of his suit coat. Rainwater's hair was almost at waist length and was drawn into multiple 'pig-tails' with leather strips binding the hair strands.

Counsel for the Board, Avery Michaels, stood, and made a respectful, near bow to the Administrative Judge.

"Your Honor, if it please the Court, I would like to raise a preliminary objection. Mr. Wells has not established his right as an attorney to appear in these proceedings. We were not provided with any information as to whether Mr. Wells is authorized to practice Law before this august body, or in the State of Maryland, at all. I have reviewed the records of the Maryland Client Protection Fund and do not see Mr. Well's name among those authorized to practice Law in the State of Maryland. And, further, there has been no 'pro hac vice' motion filed in these proceedings."

Michaels sat down and nodded smugly to the Board members seated behind him, his clients.

Wells glanced over to Michaels and then addressed the judge. "My apologies, your Honor and Mr. Michaels. I am licensed in Maryland under my birth name of Francis Weller. But my Lumbee Indian name is 'Rainwater Wells.' The actual name, translated from Croatan, is more complicated than that, but basically my family's name is intended to communicate the pleasures of a spring rain and the collection of the living waters it produces."

Several members of the Board grimaced and rolled their eyes.

Michael's legal assistant, Ashley, did a quick check online and confirmed that, indeed, Mr. Wells or Weller, was authorized to practice law in Maryland. Ashley wanted to also tell Mr. Michaels that—and this was interesting—Mr. Wells was also authorized to practice before the United States Supreme Court and had tried and won four cases there in the past seven years, but Mr. Michaels waved her away once he learned that Wells was licensed in Maryland.

Mr. Michaels responded: "Thank you for that information, Counselor. My objection is withdrawn."

Attorney Wells nodded and continued. "Your Honor, the decision to revoke and permanently suspend the medical license of my client, Doctor Alan Switzer, was flawed and constituted reversible error. Doctor Switzer has been stripped of his license due to 'a pattern of unprofessional behavior involving his habitual dependence on narcotics.' Yes, dependencies, addictions, obsessions. Doctor Switzer was a man with dependencies, some of which were alleged to be driven by narcotic drugs. But, unequivocally, not all of Doctor Switzer's dependencies were so."

Wells placed his hands behind his back and continued to stand, letting curiosity take over. A few moments of silence passed. "For example, in July of 1996, Doctor Switzer saved the life of a child already pronounced dead at the scene by drowning. The child lived, because Doctor Switzer refused to give up on her life. He was obsessed with saving the child's life. You may have read in the AMA Journal about Doctor Switzer's heroic CPR efforts and the wonderful new life that has opened up for that child, who by the way, has stated her desire to become a medical doctor, too."

Wells looked over at the Board panel seated in the courtroom. "And then, even earlier, in 1994, you may recall the incident at Glen Burnie Medical, where Doctor Switzer was uncomfortable with the Radiologist's Report in the Ogleby case. It's referenced in the record. The Radiologist found no indicia of breast cancer. But Doctor Switzer disagreed. Thanks to him, more testing was performed and a proper diagnosis, in accord with the results of Doctor Switzer's initial breast examination of the patient, were produced. But for Doctor Switzer's zeal, would Mrs. Ogleby be here among the living, today? Doubtful."

A few members of the Board were thinking back—wasn't Ogleby the complainant in a sexual battery case against Switzer? But Wells was speaking again. And he was quite interesting to watch.

"And think back to 1998, August. 'Patient Dumping,' the headline read. Yes, the Baltimore Sun had taken the medical profession to task for its cavaliere practice of allowing hospitals to 'dump' Medicaid patients onto other hospitals and medical centers that, demographically, handled the health needs of the majority of the economically challenged and disadvantaged of our Greater Maryland Community."

Avery Michaels stood briskly. "Objection. A news story of specious origin and accuracy has no bearing on the reasonableness of the Board's decision about this particular Respondent."

The Judge looked up. "Overruled."

She was enjoying Wells' performance. No need to stop, now.

Wells continued. "While practicing In Perryton, on one evening in March, 1995, Doctor Switzer visited Perryton General to make rounds. As he approached the entrance, he saw a man lying on the ground, just outside the ER entrance. He called for Emergency personnel to come out and to please assist him with bringing the patient in. But the Emergency desk personnel had been instructed to leave the patient outside. This was a 'turf war', and Perryton ER believed that it had to make a stand. They would not allow Doctor Switzer to bring the patient inside."

"Doctor Switzer immediately returned to the distressed patient and administered essential first aid and life-saving care. The victim lived, thanks to Doctor Switzer's obsession with—or call it his habitual dependency on - doing the right thing. And that is just part of the evidence I am proffering today on Doctor Switzer's behalf. There is much more but I do not wish to burden your Honor with cumulative evidence. Yes, like many good medical men and women, Doctor Switzer has had dependencies. But, as you know, good doctors strive mightily to dig themselves out of their most difficult and destructive holes, while amplifying their 'dependencies'—their obsessions—with doing good things for patients."

Switzer was thinking back that the ER guy was one of his partying buddies—he had had his ass kicked at the local pool hall—but he thought it best not to mention it at this point.

"If it please your Honor, we have submitted the most recent report of Dr. Ellen Broadbent of the Cecil County Chapter of Narcotics Anonymous. Dr. Switzer's attendance and participation in that program have been judged as 'exemplary' by Dr. Broadbent. I ask your Honor to please consider Doctor Switzer's zealous adherence to, and performance in, his N. A. program. And I ask your Honor to please consider the following: With his medical license suspended pending the outcome of this hearing, Dr. Switzer has, nevertheless, been volunteering as a technician for the midnight shift with the EMT team in Perryton, the least desirable and most challenging venue for a medical volunteer. He does so because of his obsession for doing good and helping people with medical needs and emergencies. These are the obsessions and addictions of a good man. Your Honor, please help this good doctor find his way back home again."

• • •

October 1996

"I'd like to speak with Mr. Wilson—William Wilson. Is he available?"

Ricciti had been expecting a call from one of his "investors." He barked back into the handset: "Sorry buddy—wrong number."

He was about to hang up, but then the voice mentioned a company's name and something about an insurance claim. "Well, that's not our name and we don't have any William Wilson working here and we haven't filed any insurance claims. So... sorry pal."

But the voice was telling him that "Wilson" had to be correct and that if he checked the business filing with the State for his own company, he'd see that "William Wilson" was the resident agent for his company. That he must know that, right? And, if he would check further, he would see that Proximity Estates, LLC must be a related company because it was located at the exact same address and in the same exact office suite and with the exact same resident agent, William Wilson, and that he would like to speak with William Wilson. And then the voice was saying that this was a follow-up on the insurance claim filed by William Wilson on a property owned by Proximity Estates.

Ricciti was confused. "An insurance claim? What kind?" The voice said, "fire."

"Fire—like a house fire? What was that address?" The voice repeated the address.

"Ok buddy—give me your name again and number and I'll check this out and get back to you."

Ricciti scribbled down the info. He hung up the phone. What the hell was going on?

• • •

November 20, 1996

He was angry and afraid. But more afraid than angry. Palanzo had been borrowing his mom's car. He figured that Willoughby would have easily recognized his teal, 1995 Mustang, but not a copper, 1987 Camry. It was 3:30 AM and here he was trailing the filthy gutter rat, allegedly their 'partner,' into an unbelievably ugly part of West Side. He thought the last neighborhood, lined with graffiti-covered, boarded-up houses, was the worst he had ever seen in his life. He was now rolling quietly into an even more miserable side street. Had he been informed that a bomb had been detonated here, he wouldn't have doubted it. That anyone could call this place 'home' made him feel physically ill.

He had surreptitiously followed Willoughby for three consecutive nights after work. He hadn't been sleeping anyway, so why not? He hadn't told Lou. He had overheard Willoughby and Tex in a shouting match a few days back. And then Tex must have cut and run because Tex had not been in the office for several days, which was very unusual. Something was going on.

Tonight, he followed Willoughby to a bar in East Baltimore. This was different than Willoughby's forays into the Block the past two nights. Outside the bar, Willoughby met up with a big white guy and a lanky Rastafarian with dreads. They all piled into the white guy's maroon Coup Deville and made their way into this war zone. Palanzo was pretty sure he had not been spotted. He dared not follow too closely into the side street—his car would surely be noticed. He pulled over and waited to see where the Deville would go.

It stopped about a third of the way down the street, in front of a boarded-up, partially caved-in rowhouse. The nearest functioning street lamp was nearly a half block away. Three shadowy figures disembarked from the Deville. The street was otherwise dead.

The big guy went and unlocked the trunk. Palanzo saw Willoughby and the Rastafarian looking in. Suddenly, what had been hushed tones turned into a clamor. The Rastafarian was arguing loudly with the big guy. Palanzo could hear him say "No way, mon! No fucking way!" He saw Willoughby's frame jostling—he was laughing. There were more hushed sounds from the big guy who was pointing to the car, telling the Rasta to get back into the car and to shut the fuck up. He saw the Rasta arguing some more, less loudly. But the big guy got up in his face and poked him with his finger in the chest several times. He saw the Rasta shake his head and get back into the car.

Then he saw Willoughby and the big guy pull a long sack, like something wrapped in sheets, from the trunk. It was heavy because they struggled getting it out. They took it to the front door of the house. But there was no actual door. It was rotting plywood.

Willoughby dropped his part of the weight onto the ground. The big guy continued to hold his end. Willoughby delivered a fierce kick to the plywood which immediately gave way. He kicked a few more times to further open the chasm and peeled back splintered wood, chucking it aside. He then picked up his end of the load and the two moved the load into the house.

A minute or so passed and Palanzo saw the two come back out through the hole. They went back to the open trunk.

Willoughby jammed a flashlight into his pants pocket, and each of them grabbed two large red plastic containers with handles. The containers were heavy and the big guy struggled with two. He took just one, leaving the other on the sidewalk. Willoughby looked back and laughed. He heard him say, "pussy."

The big guy eventually came back for the other container and went back in. And then he came right back out and got into the driver's side of the Deville.

About five minutes later, Willoughby came out without any cans. He got in the passenger side and the car quietly rolled away.

Palanzo waited a minute to let them get out of sight. He followed in their direction but was distracted by the bright light in his rearview mirror. He braked and craned his head to look out the back window. The house was on fire. He blinked a few times turning back around to look in the rearview and then craned his neck back around again. Yes. The flames had quickly engulfed the building. His hands shaking, he grasped the wheel and pushed the accelerator, gently. He quietly drove away, back to home.

• • •

September 13, 2015

Detective Sergeant Boyce phoned Dixit's cell.

"Kev—are you on duty?"

Boyce used his most coaxing delivery. He knew Dixit was not on duty. It was Sunday morning. Dixit had already worked about 40 minutes past his shift trying to get rid of Detective Dinetta Laurence. It was her third day on the job as a detective and she would not stop talking about their cases. He knew how she felt. He was like that too, once.

"Well sure, Sarg. What's up?"

He looked over at Laurence. She would probably like this,

whatever it was.

"Surprise—a homicide. But a citizen, female, in Roland Park."

Dixit understood. He was the "go to" detective for dealing with Baltimore's white taxpayers. The brass soon learned to send Dixit out if they wanted to avoid receiving the usual wrath of shit from privileged, politically-connected, white citizens. Other cops were deemed "too insensitive."

Laurence was looking over, anxiously, from the passenger seat, hoping for more work.

A few minutes later they were pulling into the driveway of a massive, faux Tudor mansion placed at the end of a cul-de-sac.

Dixit smiled. "Just like that house-breaking in Mondawmin."

No response.

Dixit was still trying to figure out if Dinetta Laurence had a sense of humor. Apparently not. He had tried to kid with her, a little, yesterday. He told about his old boss, Hayman. Hayman used to always say, "identifying the killer is easy. All you have to do is find the last person to see the victim alive." Laurence didn't get it.

He told her about the other thing Hayman used to say, "why didn't they throw the guy in jail when they were taking his picture for 'wanted poster?'" No response.

Dixit pulled in next to the mobile crime lab. He saw the patrol car parked across the street next to the Medical Examiner's wagon. Several curious dog-walking neighbors had congregated on the sidewalk in front of the home.

Dixit and Laurence met Officer Latrobe in the living room.

"Hey Detectives. A weird one. Female. Caucasian. Late 40's. Owner. Mrs. Joyce Elsrode. Stabbed in the chest in her art studio out back. Like a garage or shed. The M.E. and crime lab are back there."

A middle-aged woman was sitting on the hardwood staircase, sobbing gently into her crossed arms. A uniformed, female officer stood next to her, trying to comfort her.

"That's Johnstone with Mrs. Marilyn Espinosa. With an 'S.' She's the housekeeper. She found the victim. Mrs. Espinosa arrived at around 8 AM and after letting herself in and not seeing or hearing her boss, she went back to the art studio. She knocked with no response, so she used her key and went in. That's about all we got."

Latrobe looked around anxiously.

Dixit noticed. "You guys are off shift?"

"I am, but not Johnstone."

"Sure, get on home. We'll pick it up."

"Thanks Detective. Kind of weird back there. There's a lot of art and shit...."

They walked over to Johnstone and the grieving Mrs. Espinosa.

"Mrs. Espinosa, I'm Detective Kev Dixit and this is Detective Dinetta Laurence."

Mrs. Espinosa raised her head and blinked away her tears.

"We're going to borrow Officer Johnstone for a little while. Officer Laurence is going to stay and talk with you. She'll ask you some background information on Mrs. Elsrode, too." Dixit looked over towards Johnstone. "Officer, could you please head out front and manage the neighbors? See if any of them have any information that may be helpful. Names and phone numbers. And if you need any help, go ahead and radio-in."

"Yes Detective. Do you want me to lay down tape, maybe along the hedge at the entrance?"

"Yes, please. If you could wrap it all along the front part, there, okay? Thanks."

Dixit exited through the front entrance and walked towards the mossy, slate pathway leading along the side of the house to the back yard. He looked down at the path and hesitated before taking a step. He would have tried to walk only on the slate pavers, but then figured that shoe prints may have also impressed themselves onto the mossy growth on the slate—which should be preserved. But, as he hesitated, two members of the Crime Lab came along the pathway in the opposite direction towards him.

"It's ok Detective—we already got what we could from there. The witness and Latrobe had walked all over it anyway. That's the problem with a crime scene—you can't know it is one until you've trampled it."

Dixit chuckled. "Do you need me to suit-up?"

"No. We are basically done. Gloves are fine."

Dixit went into the breast pocket of his navy blue sports coat and snapped on a pair of latex gloves.

The slate pavers wound around the side of the home to the back yard. The stones ended abruptly at an ancient concrete path, partially hidden in the ground. Dixit inhaled and smelled the fragrances of an English garden to the left, wildly overgrown with herbs and ferns. Across from the garden, a goldfish pond gurgled, gently. The slimy backs of the bulbous goldfish shimmered along the surface of the water. The concrete pathway re-emerged at the entrance of the art studio, which Dixit figured was probably a large potting shed in an earlier incarnation.

The door was open, and he stood back waiting for the Crime Lab photographer to finish taking shots just inside the entrance.

"Oh sorry, Detective. We're almost done."

As Dixit waited, he tried the doorknob of the open door and saw that it was set to lock automatically whenever the door closed.

He entered and saw the M. E., Pulverton, crouching down over the body, firmly applying his gloved hands to the victim's torso. With his 70's style hair, he always reminded Dixit of a cheesy lounge pianist, teleported from a Vegas bar.

Pulverton looked up. "Hey Dixit. Not surprised to see you here."

"Yeah—white meat is my specialty."

Dixit took a look around at the chaos. Paintings, canvases, brushes and tubes of paint had been tossed onto the floor of the studio at random. An easel lay collapsed in the middle of the studio floor, with an overturned canvas nearby. A camera tripod lay on its side with its legs still extended.

Crime Lab personnel were working from their portable bench finishing-up their bagging and logging.

He saw the crumpled body of a thin woman in a long gingham dress, lying on her side. Her blood had seeped onto the hard, clay floor. Overhead, florescent lights buzzed gently.

"From what I can tell, she took a knife to the heart. Probably severed a ventricle. Feels like just one stab. No repeats. Which is a little weird. She's probably been dead since around 10 or 11 last night."

"Ok. Did you roll her, yet?"

"Yeah, after the lab guys did their thing, of course."

Dixit thought, 'yes, I know that you know how to do your job Pulverton, geez.'

"So, I think the killer was face to face with her and gave her one hard punch with the knife." Pulverton made an upward motion with his right hand, approximating the thrust.

"Almost lucky—or unlucky—the way the killer jabbed the knife right underneath the rib cage, straight into the heart. There are a hundred ways to take a knife wound to the chest and survive.

This was not one of them." Dixit nodded. He looked over to a Crime Lab tech. "Hey, Choke? Have you logged-in the weapon, yet? Can I see it?"

"Yeah—hey Kev."

The technician handed over the marked, plastic evidence bag to Dixit. It contained a sturdy palette knife with a long triangular blade. Blood had smeared onto the insides of the plastic bag. Dixit instinctively looked around the studio to see if any other palette knives were around. He saw a few flung around towards the back of the shed.

Pulverton was standing up now, stretching.

"You can see that the length of the palette knife was a factor. Had it been an inch or inch and a half shorter it may not have been lethal."

Dixit nodded. He stooped back down closer to the body and looked at the woman's face. Her features expressed a calmness that belied the attack she had suffered.

"Choke—did you bag a purse—a phone?"

"Sure, take a look."

Dixit stood and checked-out the bagged evidence on the Crime Lab bench.

"What's in the purse?" Dixit held up the marked bag.

The tech opened a file on his laptop. "A cell phone, tissues, car keys and two additional keys on a ring and a smaller purse holding cosmetics, $73.28 in cash, an electronic key card, driver's license, six credit cards, three small photos, a voter's card and a health insurance card."

"Ok, there's a tripod over there. Did you bag a camera?"

"No—no camera."

"Did she have jewelry?"

"Yep, just a wedding ring and engagement ring. We bagged

it."

"Ok, I know you guys are really busy, but when you get it back, I'm really going to need that thumb, asap."

"Well, it's Sunday, so probably late tomorrow or Tuesday." Seeing Dixit scowl, he added: "Of course, we'll prioritize."

Pulverton spoke up. "This has been dandy, guys. But can we cart the victim out of here, now?"

"Sorry Pulv—hang on for just another minute. Laurence needs to see this. Let me get her."

He had learned a long time ago that women saw things differently than men. And they usually saw things that men did not.

As he approached the front of the home, he saw that Johnstone had called-in back-up. A second uniform was keeping the expanding group of curiosity seekers at bay. He saw a man among the onlookers waving his arms, trying to get Dixit's attention. The man was speaking to Johnstone who then looked back towards Dixit. Dixit ignored the man and motioned Johnstone over to the front of the home.

"Who's that guy?"

"Says his name is Trimble—the family's lawyer."

"Already? Great, just what we need. Tell him to hang tight and I'll be right over. And then could you come back inside and stay with Mrs. Espinosa?"

• • •

Laurence stretched on a white latex glove with her other, already gloved hand as she and Dixit walked back towards the studio. "What did you get from Mrs. Espinosa?"

Laurence pulled a small notebook out of her pants pocket. But she kept walking and didn't look at the notebook. "Mrs. Elsrode, Joyce, was Philip Elsrode's second wife. Philip Elsrode had divorced his first wife and then met Joyce at a 'singles' cooking class. They were married about three years ago. She was mid-40's, he was mid-60's. But Philip Elsrode died six months ago from pancreatic cancer. Mrs. Espinosa said it was hard for Joyce because Joyce was had never experienced loss of a loved one from cancer. It was a home hospice situation and really tough on her."

Dixit was thinking, "and even tougher for him" but, considering Laurence's sense of humor, didn't bother to verbalize it.

"Any enemies? Financial problems—family problems?"

"Not according to Mrs. Espinosa. 'Everyone loved Dr. Elsrode.' He was a retired dentist with money. His ex-wife is remarried and living in Hawaii. Joyce and Philip had no kids of their own. Joyce's son from her first marriage is married and living in the Midwest somewhere. No other kids. No known or obvious enemies."

"Did Mrs. Elsrode have a new boyfriend, etc.?"

Laurence looked towards her notepad, but kept walking and did not actually consult it. "No. She had pretty much been surrounded by people from her church group and her art students during and after Philip's illness. Her church people had become her emotional support."

As they entered the studio, Pulverton introduced himself. "I run the meat wagon, Detective."

He held out his gloved hand. The unamused, gloved hand of Dinetta Laurence clasped his and shook, politely. "I'm done, so take a look around—but don't take anything!"

Laurence ignored the comment. "Call me when you're ready."

Pulverton shook his head left for some fresh air.

Laurence looked around at the chaos and walked over, respectfully, to Mrs. Elsrode's body. She knelt down and felt the gingham dress with a gloved hand.

Dixit was hanging back near the entrance. "Pulverton said she took a knife through the sternum into the heart. He thinks just one thrust. It was a palette knife. What do you make of this mess?"

Detective Laurence stood up and carefully walked around the jumble on the floor, trying not to step on any evidence. She picked-up a canvas lying near the overturned easel. A landscape—a floral arrangement. She picked up another. A more abstract work, looking like a 1930's electric toaster, but on fire—almost. She raised one more canvas from the floor. A portrait of a child, unfinished.

"Wow, a lot of different styles here. I think she was good."

Dixit thought, 'great—wasn't looking for art criticism,' but kept his mouth shut.

Laurence continued poking around. "Did she have a purse or wallet? Jewelry? Car keys? Is her car here?"

"Purse, jewelry and keys are accounted for. Good question about the car. I assumed it was that Cabriolet out front—but we'll need to ask Mrs. Espinosa."

Laurence walked over to tipped-over tripod.

"She must have been taking photos. Did they find a camera?"

"No, no camera."

Laurence lifted up the tripod from the floor. She saw that a glob of sticky cellophane tape was stuck to the screw port for the camera. She was thinking that it must have been broken.

Dixit smirked. "So, what do you think, Detective? Is this your first 'locked room' mystery?"

Laurence looked up. "Locked room?"

"Yes, you know the classic 'movie of the week.' The victim is found alone in a locked room. How did the killer do it?"

Dixit was trying not to smile.

Laurence was wondering what a 'movie of the week' was.

"Remember—Mrs. Espinosa told us she used her key to enter the studio. So, it was locked. How did the killer get out? How did the killer get in?"

Laurence saw the gleam in Dixit's eyes. They had warned her about his 'alleged' sense of humor. "Through the door?"

Dixit was smiling, now. He couldn't help it.

"Did the killer murder the woman and lock the door behind?"

Laurence went towards the entrance.

"I'm guessing it's set to lock behind, automatically. Here you go."

She tried the doorknob.

"Yes, he walked out and it locked behind him."

"Excellent! So how did the killer get in if the door was locked?"

Laurence knew that Dixit was messing with her, but figured it was safer to go along with the eccentric.

"Well, presuming that Mrs. Elsrode was locked in, he either had a key, or the victim let him in."

Dixit smiled again. "Why is it a 'he?'"

Laurence was thrown off and a little mad at herself. She had reverted to cop sexism. But she rallied.

"Well, you're right Detective. I spoke in a conclusory fashion. The killer obviously could be male or female—or anything in between."

"Ok, sorry Detective, I'm just messing with you. This is the kind of shit that my old boss, Hayman, used to pull on me all the time when I first joined CID. Just remember, we have a lot of assholes in CID. They like to mess with the newbies a little."

Laurence looked at Dixit with a 'and I care because?' look.

Dixit sighed. "Ok, what is your sense of this?"

"Well, I guess we're supposed to believe that someone went berserk in here as part of a killing rampage. But one knife wound to the chest is not much of a rampage. And robbery, at least of the usual stuff, is certainly not the motive."

Dixit nodded, approvingly. Laurence finally put her notepad back in her pocket and continued.

"Presuming Joyce was locked in, the killer either had a key or was invited in. Either one of those suggests she knew the killer and that this was a crime of passion. The palette knife was likely a weapon of opportunity. Something happened between two people here last night that led to a murder. The 'crazy' crime scene was probably a weak attempt at staging by an amateur killer."

• • •

September 14, 2015

Dixit hadn't slept much. As usual, the murder had taken over. There was a lot to consider.

Dixit and Laurence looked like all good detectives do following assignment to a high-profile murder case: beat to hell or hungover—or both. And the fact that it was a Monday morning didn't help. They were sipping acrid-smelling coffee out of white Styrofoam cups in the so-called 'conference room,' a dilapidated, rectangular cubicle within the bullpen. Halogen lights burned down brightly on their scalps. Laurence had slept less than Dixit. Adrenaline had kept her brain going most of the night. Her husband, James, was trying to get used to the new routine. He was taking a lot more shifts with the baby. He was not loving life.

"So, I'd like you to handle the case briefing this morning. I'll chime in as needed. Can you?"

Laurence looked up like a deer in the headlights, but quickly adjusted. "Yes, Detective. I definitely can." It was her fourth day as a detective. She had seen the case briefings on the other mornings and knew what to expect. She could do it.

"Good. Let me bring you up to speed. First, the attorney, Trimble. The guy was quite a trip. He told me about thirty times that attorney-client privilege prevented him from commenting and then proceeded to comment, endlessly. I couldn't shake him."

Laurence grabbed her notepad.

"Like you said, no known enemies. No known boyfriends. She gave art lessons to a bunch of people, but currently just two senior citizens and one of their grandkids. Socialized with her church people. Trimble knew both of the Elsrodes, professionally and socially. I asked about Mrs. Elsrode's will—who would gain financially from her death. He said everything would go to Joyce's son, Jack—last name Donnelly—who Trimble said had been informed and would be flying out here from Chicago in a couple days. According to Trimble, their relationship was good, but we'll need to check him out, of course.

Laurence was writing notes, furiously. Dixit paused a second to give Laurence a moment to catch-up.

"We have to eliminate theft as a motive—I know, not likely— but it has to be checked out, so I asked Trimble if he would help us to take a look around the house and studio to see if he could think of anything significant that may have been stolen. The killer could have worked their way through the house, first, before confronting Mrs. Elsrode in the studio. Trimble said that if the killer used a key to access the studio, it would not have worked in the home. The home has a high-tech lock and alarm system. You need an electronic key to gain access. The studio key is just a simple, old-school key. Trimble confirmed that the housekeeper had the electronic key and would let herself in on working mornings.

He didn't think anyone else, besides Mrs. Elsrode had the house key. And we know she had a studio key. But I'll get Trimble back to the house later this morning to check things out. We've got the names of the three art students. Trimble said he would work on a list of her church friends."

Laurence chimed-in: "Mrs. Espinosa confirmed that the Cabriolet was Joyce's."

"Ok, good—that eliminates that. Now for the exciting news. Forensics texted me ten minutes ago to tell me that the victim's phone had been wiped clean of prints."

Dixit paused so that the news could sink in.

Laurence stopped scribbling and looked up. After a few moments she spoke. "Ok, that tells us that the killer took the phone, possibly to learn something by reading her texts and emails—maybe listening to her voicemails. Or maybe he took the phone to delete evidence? A prior communication from the killer that the killer had to delete?"

"Yes, that's what I'm thinking. Any or all of those."

"Do we have the thumb drive, yet, with the stuff from the phone?" Laurence was thinking that Dixit probably hadn't worked the Crime Lab sufficiently to get fast results. She assumed it was a bunch of old guys like Dixit, taking their time.

Dixit smiled. "We will have the thumb drive in approximately a half hour. We have friends."

Laurence nodded; she felt a little foolish. Dixit continued.

"We'll start with a two-week timeline. When we get the thumb, I'd like you to check through all the emails, texts, the call log, photos, web searches—all the stuff from the last two weeks. Create a spreadsheet timeline with all of the players in contact with the victim during that time according to the phone data. Make a list and prioritize by frequency of contact within the two-week period. We will cross-check the list with the names that Trimble gives us. When you handle this briefing, tell them what you're doing and that we'll need at least two more of us to help. I'm thinking Quint and Bonaventure. Split the work four ways. We'll need to get interviews started asap and start checking and cross-checking alibis."

Laurence finished her frantic note-taking and picked up her lipstick-stained Styrofoam cup for a sip. The vile substance produced an unpleasant puckering effect. She noticed her hand shaking but steadied herself.

• • •

Tuesday September 15, 2015

Detective Laurence, again, took the podium for the team briefing. Morale was beginning to sink. They had gotten nowhere in 48 hours. Dixit stood a few yards away with Boyce, giving Laurence her space.

"If you hadn't heard—and I'm guessing everyone here has—bad news about the phone. When Forensics told us that it had been wiped clean of prints, we knew the killer had taken the phone, most likely to read and then delete any incriminating text message or email. We know that all that stuff is stored by the internet service provider on its servers, anyway, so that all we have to do is take a look at the stuff on the servers to see what was deleted. The perps don't always know this. So, Detective Dixit was able to get the attorney, Trimble, to get appointed Executor on an expedited basis yesterday so that Trimble could consent to our access to the victim's phone data. But we discovered that no texts, emails or search history had been deleted from the phone. The call log was not altered. Nothing. And we also checked the victim's stored photos. She had used her phone to photograph her paintings. The victim had cloud back-up so, all of her photos were also available from the internet service provider. The photos on the server and her phone consist entirely of her art work. There is no photo of a person or any other thing or place that shows up on the server but not on the phone. It's all her art work. So, although the perpetrator may have checked-out the phone, there likely was nothing incriminating and worth deleting. So, this unfortunately looks like a dead end."

Dixit jumped in. "And, yeah of course, we're on a two-week timeline for now. We've got emails and texts from about a dozen people. These are all people Detectives Quint and St. Bonaventure and ourselves are interviewing. A lot these are her church friends. And that makes sense as they had been the ones helping Mrs. Elsrode all along while her husband was ill. There's nothing unusual in the content to suggest some motive for killing. And we've got the grandparent art students emailing—just scheduling and assignment stuff. Nothing suspicious. So, we're going to wrap up with this group and dig deeper and expand our timeline. And we're going to have to double check all imperfect spousal alibis. So, we need some more bodies on this. Who's got availability?"

The room of tired looking plainclothes uniformly slouched down in their chairs, trying to hide. At 6 feet 2 and 210 pounds, former kickboxing champ Tangela Smith was a little hard to miss.

"Smith, are you still on the 'Orpheus?'"

Smith sighed. "Yes, Chief, but if you need maybe six to eight hours from me in the next couple days, I am all yours."

"Good. Thanks. Quint and St. Bonaventure—see me and Laurence at the end of this and we'll get you started on the next batch. Tangela, catch up with those two later and take who they assign."

Back in the conference cubicle, the four sat under the searing halogen lamps.

Dixit addressed the three. "Ok at this point we have to focus on anything unusual you may have gotten from your interviews. Anything odd? Anything just 'off?'"

Quint was thinking it odd that such a group of old people could uniformly have such bad breath, but figured she would keep that to herself. Instead, she said, "nothing, Chief. Mostly very nice old Methodists. They reminded me of my grandparents."

Bonaventure chimed in. "Same here, Kev. And they all love those two priests or whatever they call them. Especially the younger guy, Singletary. He brings the shut-ins communion on Sundays. But nothing unusual."

Quint spoke up. "Ha! Yeah, well I know one of the old ladies that wasn't so in love with him. She said that when he came over that Sunday morning with communion, he had forgotten his key and couldn't let himself in—so she had to get out of her chair and make her way to the door with her walker, which was apparently a big deal for her. She said she had given him her key so that he could let himself in on Sundays and save her the hassle. She bitched and moaned at me as though I could do something."

Bonaventure smiled. "Ah, yes, and one of them told me the older guy's sermons were too long and could we get him to shorten them!"

Dixit shook his head. "You should have reminded them about the 'separation of church and state.' Anything else? C'mon—nothing?"

• • •

July, 2001

He couldn't help himself. On seeing Ricciti seated behind the plexiglass, he cupped his hands together and let out an incredibly long, strident whistle that bounced all over the stark, uncomfortable room.

The sound blew through the cheesy microphone in the plexiglass causing Ricciti to physically flinch in his seat. The guard outside peered quickly through the port window of the door. But then, the whistling noise stopped.

Ricciti inhaled, brushed back his stringy blond hair and adjusted his wire framed glasses. "Jesus Christ, Skip—you fuckin' scared the living shit out of me with that!"

Weller laughed: "I know, I know—I still love doing that to people!"

Ricciti took a closer look through the glass. "What the fuck happened to you Weller—what's with the crazy-assed outfit?"

"Well, I never mentioned it to anyone back in the day, but I'm actually a Native American. A Lumbee."

"Really?"

"Yeah, really. This is me."

"Ok man—it's cool. And thank you for giving a shit about me and Pete. We've been royally fucked over. Whether you can do anything for us or not—thank you, one way or another. I mean it, Skip—thank you."

"Well, I might have something. But it's a Hail Mary. I don't want to give you guys false hope. My idea may be shit. But do you remember when the U.S. Attorney dropped all of your charges except for RICO, which you pled to?"

He wasn't sure because he never knew exactly what his previous attorney was doing. "Uh, sure."

"Ok. I asked both of your attorneys to provide me with all of the discovery material in the cases. Of course, even though you both appointed me your counsel, neither attorney felt inclined to assist. So, I had to threaten to have them disbarred. And, of course, then they sent it over very quickly. I could tell they hadn't even looked at most of it. A lot of it had never been removed from the envelopes and folders the feds sent. Your attorneys may have missed something important—which could help you now, but which probably would not have helped you, then."

Ricciti didn't know what Weller was talking about but kept listening.

"Remember the guy from the States Attorney's office? He filed the original charges—all Maryland stuff: theft, embezzlement, mortgage fraud, conspiracy. And then at some point the feds got their hands on it. The U.S. Attorney—Wilhelm—took over and added the RICO charges. That's their thing - their knee jerk 'go to' filing. They use RICO on the mob, gangs, financial crimes, everything. So, RICO requires that there be an effect—even minimal—on interstate commerce. But the Courts never look too closely at this requirement."

Ricciti had lost concentration. He was looking at Weller's hair braids. They were really intricate. He was thinking that Weller must have a woman because the Skip Weller he knew could never have done those. Weller could barely keep his shoe strings tied in high school.

Weller saw Ricciti looking on, blankly.

"Ok, I'm sorry Lou. I'm going too 'lawyer' on you. So, let me get to the bottom line. You guys banked, locally, right—with that bank in Little Italy?"

"Yeah. Everyone does."

"You sent all the loan applications and contracts to Scott Jansen on Eastern Avenue?"

"Yeah. But sometimes when we'd get busy, we'd drive them over to his home in Sparrows Point."

"Ok. Did you ever try to get clients outside of Maryland?"

"No. Should we have?"

"No—did you ever phone Chalk in his New York City office?"

"No. We hated the guy. Why would we?"

"How about other phone calls in or out of Maryland to and from other States?"

"No. I don't think so. Our business was all local."

"Did you ever travel to New York or outside Maryland for your business?"

"New York? Why the hell would anyone ever want to go to that shithole? That asshole Willoughby once told us that Otto fuckin' Chalk wanted us to haul our asses up there to meet with him to explain ourselves as to why we were not producing more flips. He said Chalk wanted to meet us in Central Park at some boathouse for lunch. I told Willoughby 'fuck that.' We were not going to some shitty boathouse to get our asses killed and dumped in some slime pond in Central Park, home of perverts and murderers. So, of course, we never went. Hell, Pete and I have barely been out of the State of Maryland. Well, once we were both in the Cub Scouts and were going to go on a bus trip to Cooperstown for the Hall of Fame, but I got stung really bad by fucking yellow jackets when we were playing ball. So, I couldn't go. Pete went."

Weller looked on, stunned.

"And, one time, my dad took the long way around to get to the Ocean through Delaware, because he was fed up with the Bay Bridge, but it took too fuckin' long and we never tried that again..."

"Ok—did you, as a business, ever mail anything to another state? An advertisement, a loan package to a lender, anything?"

"No—why would we? We can't handle properties in another state. My business license was here in Maryland. Pete, too, although he was licensed as an appraiser."

"Ok—that's what all the discovery material indicated. You never did any interstate commerce. Almost every business does, somehow, whether they mean to or not. So, what happened was, Wilhelm dropped every Maryland charge—because he didn't want to taint his federal prosecution, which he had stolen from the Maryland States Attorney. All that was left was the RICO stuff. But he never informed the Judge that there was no evidence of your involvement in activities of any sort beyond state lines. All the underlying charges on State crimes were gone. There were no other federal charges. Just RICO. So Wilhelm, knowingly, or maybe in ignorance, took a plea that was, technically, baseless."

"Wow, ok. So, what does that mean for me and Pete? Can we appeal?"

"Well, it's not an appeal, but I will file something called a 'writ of habeas corpus' which, basically, is a call to produce you guys to stand before a judge to let the judge hear how you have been imprisoned, wrongfully. It gives us a shot to let a federal judge see what happened in your cases. The judge could set you free. The downside is if we win, your plea bargain will be stricken and you may have to stand trial again. Or, the U.S. Attorney's Office may figure you've done about the same time you'd have done under a reasonable plea bargain and not bother. And I'm thinking the State has other things on their radar, too, and may not bother, either. You've both done over 18 months for a low-level, white-collar crime, with asset forfeiture. I think you might wind up free. But all of this is a long shot."

"Well, shit! Let's do it, Skip!"

• • •

Weller listened to the gravel crunch and squeak beneath his boots as he walked back through the visitor's parking lot to his car. He looked down at his shadow as he walked. It was short, today, in the midday sun. And hot as hell. His black suit made it feel all the hotter.

He wondered if Ricciti and Palanzo even knew that Chalk was dead? Chalk was found taking a comfortable bath in his Manhattan penthouse with both wrists slit. But the polite suicide was eventually revised to homicide when the autopsy report came back indicating death by asphyxiation. The other one, Birckhead, had moved to Kentucky to engage in even more brazen financial crimes. She was now doing time in Pewee Valley courtesy of the Kentucky Correctional Institution for Women. He had read that she was bitching and moaning about unfair treatment of women executives. The guy Jansen had turned state's evidence and had done no time at all. He was a golf pro now. No one had ever tracked down the other ones. They had gotten away with it somehow.

• • •

January, 1999

They saw the guy in the navy-blue sports coat and grey slacks. He was smiling, very much at ease, just wandering around the bullpen. He gently waved and mouthed a quiet 'hello' as he passed each cubicle. At least he respected Mondays. No one liked Mondays. Quiet was critically important to the CID cops on Monday mornings. Hangovers, break-ups and insomnia were the foul aftertastes of the preceding Saturday and Sunday.

Was this guy the new "Hey Mon?" He looked Jamaican—maybe.

Hayman had sent the last new guy, Aurelio De Hidalgo St.

Bonaventure, aka "Hey Mon," packing. Word was he would never have cut it in the CID under Hayman. The team of "Hayman and 'Hey Mon'" was short-lived. St. Bonaventure had been a sociology major. He was promoted into the CID because he had a 'Jamaican' accent. The brass thought that, undercover, he could pass as a street level Jamaican gang banger in the West Side. St. Bonaventure knew better. He was Bajan. His family had emigrated from Barbados when he was a teenager. They were all naturalized, U.S. citizens. St. Bonaventure was urbane and well-educated. He could never pass for the raw, street level murderers planted in the West Side by the Jamaican drug mob. To the average Baltimorean, his Bajan dialect was no different than a Jamaican accent. To the Jamaicans, he was a lily-white English professor. He was meat. He had somehow found his way back to Patrol and away from Hayman. He might actually live.

Stan Hayman rolled into his chair in the bullpen. He was the oldest, most feared, and detested Detective in CID; he was a boozer—and an ugly one. He was in a constant state of hangover. Beyond 'a little overweight,' his gut hung perilously over his 'sans a belt,' double-knit slacks. The pants were part of a leisure suit, purchased at a clearance sale at Caldor's in 1981. He had left the jacket behind in an East Baltimore bar, somewhere, sometime, maybe a decade before.

Dixit saw that his new boss had arrived so he approached, cheerily, his right arm extended for a 'good morning' handshake. Hayman saw the smiling, foreign man approaching and remembered, great—today was 'a new guy.'

Hayman quickly barked: "Kid—run down to the canteen and get me a large coffee. The largest. You know, the biggest cup they have. Double sugar. Double cream. Now. I mean right now!"

Every ear perked up. Personnel sat, attentively, watching the drama unfold. There was no better form of entertainment than 'Hayman meets a rookie.'

Hayman knew that he had to put the asshole in his place. Another 'minority' promotion. It pissed him off that CID would take an Asian or Hawaiian foreigner or whatever the fuck he was, over eligible, good white guys from Baltimore.

When Assistant Commissioner Ratliff had pulled Hayman into his office to tell Hayman the 'good news,' Hayman was unsurprised. He saw a spade for a spade. It was a 'minority' promotion. So what if the guy passed some kind of aptitude test—what did Ratliff call it — the Auberge-Fleming Cognitive Creativity test. So what if he had 'the highest score ever measured' in the Department? Hayman only knew of the idiot test and the sergeant's exam. He had passed neither. This was bullshit to legitimize a minority promotion.

But the foreigner was coming back towards, him, sheepishly, gingerly.

"Boss, I was thinking that perhaps we could go to the canteen together and have a coffee—you, know, take a break, get acquainted a little. I could find out how you like to work—the best way to assist you?"

He was so damned soothing —and that damned smile. Hayman had become conscious of every set of eyes upon him. He did not want to, but he knew he would have to be 'nice.' If the asshole complained about poor treatment, it could fuck up his pension. He was only a year and two months away from retirement—if he wanted it.

"All right, sure. Let's go."

And to the surprise of the entire bullpen, Hayman wrested his tall frame and significant girth from the ragged, dilapidated office chair and stood queasily. He began walking, slowly, towards

Dixit.

Dixit waved his arm, beckoningly, welcomingly, towards Hayman. As they proceeded together towards the door, Dixit stopped, abruptly. "Chief, tell you what—since you're heading down to the canteen anyway, could you pick me up a large coffee, black? No need for both of us to go. I'll hang back here...."

Hayman's jaw dropped to the floor as his face quickly burned from orange and to red. But before Hayman could vocalize his extraordinary displeasure, Dixit said: "Just fucking with you, Chief! I'll be right back with that coffee!" He hightailed it, quickly, for the door, away from the ensuing, raucous laughter.

• • •

September 18, 2015

Dixit heard his front doorbell ring and thought 'this can't be good.' It was 7 PM.

Dixit saw the face through the window of the front door. It was Switzer.

He thought, 'shit, Bhavna is not going to like this.' She would be home any minute now with the kids. He opened the door, cautiously.

"Hey Kev, it's me, Alan! Did you recognize me? I know, I've got these muttonchops—like a 60's thing! It's my '68 comeback!"

"Hey, Alan—great to see you again! Yeah, wow—cool sideburns!"

Dixit let Switzer enter. He was thinking the 60's facial hair was a little more Manson than Elvis.

The two exchanged man hugs, but at least Switzer passed the 'sniff' test. He may have actually bathed recently.

"So, what brings you out here, my friend?"

Switzer looked around.

87

"Where's my favorite lady, Bhanza and the gang? I haven't seen them in a coon's age?"

"Bhavna? Oh, she's with the kids but they'll be back any second."

And just then Dixit heard the doorknob moving in the door. Vadin rushed in followed closely behind by Beth.

"Dad—did you get pizza? Hey Uncle Alan!"

Bhavna followed behind and saw Switzer. She looked less than happy.

"Oh, Alan? How nice to see you again! It's been so long..." There was an awkward pause. "Kev, could you come help me in the kitchen?"

And then, Dixit felt his cell vibrating. This was now an official dumpster fire. He looked at the phone. Laurence. Shit. He would have to take the call. Sensing imminent domestic danger, he quickly recalibrated.

"Hon, Alan and I are going out for tacos. Can we bring you something back? And I got the pizza for you guys—it's in the fridge. I picked it up a couple hours ago, ok? Should be great once you heat it up!"

He looked on pleadingly as his cell vibrated for the third time. He heard Beth yell 'yay!'

Switzer was confused but thinking that tacos would be great!

Bhavna performed a barely perceptible head shake. "Sure, boys—enjoy your tacos."

Dixit ushered Switzer out the front door and quickly picked up the call.

"Detective, it's Laurence. I think I fucked up."

He was trying to focus on what Laurence was saying but Switzer was talking at the same time.

"Great idea for tacos, Kev. I'm kind of hungry, so great idea!"

Dixit held up his hand to stop Switzer from speaking, performing an impromptu papal blessing.

"How so, Dinetta—what's happened?"

"Well, I spoke with Mrs. Espinosa again about the art students. She mentioned that the students used to drop-off their assignments—paintings and drawings—at the art studio. So I said, 'did they drop them off when Mrs. Elsrode was home?' and she says, 'no, they would drop them off anytime.'"

Switzer began speaking again. "You know, if you'd prefer Indian, that's fine too, Kev. But tacos are great if it's really what you want. But don't get tacos just on my account."

Dixit signaled a 'thumbs-up' and turned away, jamming the phone to his ear.

"Repeat that again, Dinetta—what?"

"Ok, sorry—so I said 'they left them outside the studio somewhere?' and she says 'no, they used the other key.' There's another key Kev. It's kept hidden in the garden under a rock."

Dixit thought: 'Shit.'

"Ok, that's good Laurence—very good. You did good—not a fuck-up. Did you bag it?"

"Yes—I've got it and am going to get it over to evidence. Kev, I said to her, 'why didn't you tell us before about this key?' and she said, 'you didn't ask.' I should have asked."

"No, that's ok—don't worry, we try to ask the right questions, but we can't read peoples' minds, ok?"

"Thanks, Kev. But I know I fucked up."

"No. I really don't think so. We've already interviewed the very people who would know about the key, right? Changes nothing. Let it go. We'll regroup tomorrow."

• • •

December 31, 1995

Robert Mortenson had been hearing a sound. An annoying sound. There it was again. It was like a screech—a whistling noise, almost. Piercing. But there was no teapot in the guest area in the basement. What the hell was it? And then he realized, of course, it had to be the "suitor." The damn guy had not been in the house for ten minutes and there were already problems.

At Karen's urging, he had relented and allowed Barbara to invite the guy to stay over for New Year's Eve. Barbara thought it would be good for the three to get better acquainted. It looked like things might be getting "serious." They could all share a quiet evening looking through the family photo albums followed by a Champagne toast at midnight.

But Robert did not like Chris. Chris was a pansy and his daughter was oblivious to this patently obvious fact. It was his fault. He had protected her. Karen had led a sheltered life. She never had to mix with his kind. She was an innocent. He should have explained these things to Karen. Leaving it to Barbara was a mistake. He knew what sort of creature "Chris" was. There was no future between a homosexual like Chris and his Karen. Chris was a lamprey—a leech, preying upon the good nature and financial stability of his daughter—deceiving her into thinking they could ever have a real relationship, a real life together. There would be no children. He sighed. And even worse yet, Chris was an "actor." He sighed again, more despondently. He would go downstairs to the guest room and see what the ruckus was.

Chris was busy, carefully laying-out his toiletries onto the guest vanity in the bathroom. He had left the door open and suddenly looked up to see Mr. Mortenson standing in the doorframe, scowling.

Startled, he quickly re-grouped. "Oh hey Mr. Mortenson.

Thanks again for the invitation. You, know this guest bath is really quite nice! Great décor!"

Mortenson grimaced. "Fine Chris. But just what is going on down here? What was that sound?"

Chris was puzzled. "Sound? What sound do you mean?"

"Like a piercing sound—a siren. It was coming from down here."

He thought for a moment and realized that Mr. Mortenson was speaking of his whistling. He had unconsciously been whistling a tune.

"Oh, that was probably me whistling. I think it was 'Cotton Fields.' Do you know that one?"

"What?"

"'Cotton Fields.' You know, the Lead Belly song?"

"Lead Belly? What, is that—hard rock?"

"No, no—he was like a Blues guy. Wrote a lot of classics?"

"Wonderful. But we don't whistle inside the house, ok? It's not done here. If you feel an urge to hear music, there is a perfectly fine stereo console just over there in the corner of the club basement. Help yourself. You'll find a suitable selection of Hollyridge Strings albums."

"Oh, yes—of course. Thanks Mr. Mortenson."

He was trying not to chuckle.

Mortenson peered over his spectacles and onto the vanity. He saw the two, cylindrical metallic objects—devices used by homosexual men for filthy self-gratification. It made him shudder.

"And just what do you think you're doing bringing those things into our home?" He was pointing to the vanity.

Chris was confused. "Which things?"

"Right there, those two things."

"Ah—you're probably wondering why I have two of them!"

91

Mortenson was flummoxed. "Two of them? I'm wondering how you would dare to bring even one of those things into my home. Pretty damned shameful."

"Yes, yes—I know, it's a little embarrassing but let me show you."

Mortenson felt sick and was about to tell Chris to put the damn thing down, but, too late.

Chris pulled off the top to reveal the tiny spherical cutting mechanism.

"See, I use this one for nostril hairs. I know—it's a little gross to talk about, but you seem genuinely interested. The reason I like this one is because, if you'll notice, the tip is pretty long and can really reach up into the nose. Yet, the mechanism is fairly gentle."

He reached for the other one. Mortenson had turned white.

"Now, I know it's a little odd to carry two separate trimmers, but look at this." He removed the top.

"This one has a different cutting mechanism, entirely. It's a bit shorter, too, and perfect for ear hairs, both inside and outside—that's the thing about this particular trimmer. Really good for ears, but not nearly as effective on nose hairs."

Mortenson slowly regained his composure. He shook his head in disbelief.

"I know—I don't brag about carrying two separate trimmers, but as an actor, I have to always be ready for close-ups. You just don't want to be caught with your pants down."

Mortenson had had enough. He was retreating backwards through the threshold when he spied, sitting on the vanity, a copy of his favorite magazine—the National Review—and worse yet, the brand-new issue that he had not even had a chance to read, himself! The jackass had the temerity to pinch his magazine for himself without even the decency of asking. He walked over and grabbed the magazine from the vanity, scowling.

"I'll take this, thank you."

And with that, he made his exit before a bewildered Waxley.

Chris knew that Mortenson was an odd duck, but this entire interaction was just 'off the charts' loony. He wondered whatever possessed Mortenson to take his magazine? Well, actually, it was his deceased mom's, who apparently had an endless subscription because it would always show up in his mail every month. He didn't cotton to the conservative viewpoint, but he always enjoyed reading "The Week" in the beginning of each issue. There was some pretty funny stuff there. But he was at least hoping that Mr. Mortenson would heed his advice on the trimmers. Mortenson needed some serious help in that department.

• • •

Friday, November 29, 1996

"I'm hoping we'll open this door and everything will be fine. All this shit will be gone."

Dixit and Palanzo stood behind Ricciti as he unlocked his office door. The three had just trudged up the five long flights of stairs. Being the day after Thanksgiving, they were all a little tired out by the effort.

Ricciti opened the door. Nothing had changed. The carpeting beneath the desk was steeped in blood. More blood had pooled and then dried on the office chair and desk. Blood had splattered onto the wall behind the desk, a demented Rorschach test. The corpse wore a tightly swaddled shroud of green lawn bags and duct tape. The office was cold.

"Jesus. What a fucking mess."

Dixit was just glad to see that the corpse was still there. He hadn't slept the past two nights wondering whether he had delivered a strong enough blow. He half believed that he hadn't. He felt relieved.

"Ok, let's get organized. You guys have clean-up. Pete—you said you could replace the carpet? Do you have it?"

Pete looked back, again, at the mess. He was instantly nauseous. He fought it back.

"Yeah—I brought a remnant that I can cut in here. This carpet is a lot like the stuff my dad and I installed in his office like ten years ago when he was still working. It's in my trunk."

"Good, Lou—you've got the paint?"

Lou paused and looked again at the mess. "Fuck yeah. I got paint. Sure. And many thanks to your dumb bitch who came along and did all this. Nice she's not here to help."

Dixit was shocked. He felt his blood pressure rising.

"'Dumb bitch?' Seriously? Never call her that. She's family to us!" Dixit was thinking that she had almost certainly saved his life.

Ricciti saw that he had struck a nerve and knew to back off.

"Ok, ok—sorry man, I'm just generally pissed. Sorry...."

Dixit took a breath. "Ok, Lou. It's cool." He looked at his watch.

"Brian and Chris will be over here in a couple minutes. I'll keep them downstairs on the street. You guys go ahead and get the... deceased downstairs to the lobby. Don't forget—like you said—the stairs, not the elevator, because, the security camera and time code, etc."

Ricciti shook his head. "Jesus, Kev, we got it. We're not morons."

Dixit bit-back the urge to provide an alternative viewpoint.

"Ok Lou—just making sure we have everything covered. Once the body is out, Chris, Brian and I will... have the funeral.

I'll phone you when we're done. If you need any help, I can come back here."

"We won't Kev." Ricciti was scowling.

Dixit thought, 'who the fuck's doing who the favor?' but he let it pass.

"Ok—but I'll phone you, just to be sure..."

• • •

Dixit looked out the lobby door and saw Chris and Brian leaning against a car across the street—he looked closer and saw it was Golding's hearse. Somehow, the Troll had snagged a spot right in front of the building. Dixit wound up parking almost two blocks away. Parking was scarce near the Harbor due to people being off from work and all the Black Friday sales.

Golding was taking a closer look at Waxley and the shirt under his windbreaker.

"Chris, may I ask what you are wearing, Amigo? Is that a lady's blouse or something?"

Waxley looked down at his shirt and laughed.

"This? No, this is like a tropical shirt or something. Those are dolphins and some other sea things—a tortoise, that's a bird, there, I think. It's abstract..." He was poking at his ribcage. "I found it at the Goodwill—the one in Timonium. That is an awesome place."

The Troll shook his head in disbelief. He was dressed in a black suit and tie for the occasion.

"Ok, well, at least 'Black Friday' is appropriate for a funeral."

Chris laughed. "Yeah, it always sounds so sad, but I guess it is a happy time for merchants finally getting 'in the black.'

"Yes, they should call it something like 'Happy Friday' or 'Good Friday?'"

Waxley laughed again. "You know there's already a 'Good Friday,' Troll. You do remember from your Ignatius days, right?"

"What do you mean?"

"You know—the day Christ was crucified?"

Golding had a noncommittal look on his face.

"I seem to remember something, but I'm a Jew, remember. If that is the case, why is it called 'Good Friday'? It doesn't seem to make sense. Today should be 'Good Friday,' if all the stores are doing so well. Your 'Good Friday should be 'Black Friday.' Tell your people to go arrange a swap."

Dixit arrived and the three shook hands. "Thanks again for helping out with this funeral guys. This is a big help."

"You bet, Kev. Brian has dressed the part and you're looking a little somber there, too. I wasn't thinking about a dress code. I just threw this shirt on—no tie."

"Don't worry about clothes."

The Troll jumped in. "Yeah, this guy is headed for the pauper's corner so I would not be too concerned about attire. Speaking of which, I have our very affordable $399.00 cardboard casket back there. You said the guy is lying in state up there somewhere in that building?"

"Yes, it's Palanzo and Ricciti's offices. They're bringing him down."

The Troll looked concerned. "Those two knuckleheads? Jesus Kev, I didn't realize that. You said a vagrant crept in an office and died somehow."

"Well, yeah, the guy basically wound up there where he shouldn't have been and pretty much committed suicide—or basically shot himself and died thereafter. Very sad."

"Shot himself there—in that office building? Well, that's fucked up!"

There was a long pause as Golding waited for a further explanation. There was none.

"Ok, so, like I said, as long as you get me my physician's signed death cert with raised seal and a copy of the police report, it's all good. I can do my thing."

"You bet. Here's the death cert."

Golding carefully studied the form. It looked fine. "Do you have the police report?"

"Well, being so near the holiday, it's not written up yet, but I'm the Police and I'm reporting. The guy is dead."

Golding looked suspiciously at Dixit. "Ok that's also a little fucked-up, but I trust you man."

"Thanks Brian. It's ok."

There was another awkward silence. Kev tried to make small talk. "So, Chris, what else are you working on? What's next after 'Pirates?'"

Waxley's face brightened. But he didn't dare ask whether Kev liked his TV performance on Thanksgiving. He had learned a long time ago it was best not to ask.

"Okay, well—this will sound a little off the wall, but I'm writing a play; it may wind up as a musical—I hope. Anyway, it's tough to get a great part so I figured—what the hell—I'll write myself a good part! So, the story is about two scientist friends who—well, the one guy has come up with this time travel thought experiment."

Golding muttered: "meshuggener."

"What?"

"Nothing Waxley—go ahead."

"So, it's funny, we were just talking about Good Friday— ironic. Anyway, so the one scientist is saying, 'I can prove that time travel is an impossibility and will never happen.' The other scientist says, 'how?' The first one says, 'well if you were a time traveler from the future, what event would you like to witness, firsthand?' The other scientist says, 'well, of course, any of the great events in human history.' The first scientist says, 'agreed. Wouldn't a lot of time travelers want to witness the crucifixion of Christ—an event that changed history forever?' 'Sure.' 'So, wouldn't there be a cartload of time travelers all showing up for the event?' 'Sure.' 'So, wouldn't they be just a bit conspicuous? You know, whether they appeared holographically through quantum digital means or in a more physical manifestation—even if the time travelers tried to costume themselves to blend in—they all wouldn't quite pull it off, right? There would be an awful lot of them there. And some would just not fit in?' So, the other scientist says, 'yes—what's the point?' And the first one says 'well, we've got the four books of the New Testament, chronicling the event in detail and not a single one mentions anything about a bunch of weird-looking people showing up that day and wandering around, maybe looking out of place. So, that proves that time travel will never occur, because, if it does, the New Testament writers would have observed all the time travelers that day and mentioned something.'"

Waxley paused, looking for a reaction. Nothing yet. Kev was half-listening, but looking back towards the office building. Golding was looking on with a bemused look on his face. Waxley continued.

"So, the other scientist says, 'But there was something like that.' The first one says, 'what do you mean?' The other says, 'I think it was in Matthew. Remember—the veil in the temple was torn in two and a bunch of odd-looking characters turned up who were thought to be the spirits of resurrected saints or something like that? Couldn't they be the time travelers?'"

Just then they heard a low bonking sound from the front door of the office building. They saw Palanzo and Ricciti struggling with the body, trying to maneuver it out the front glass doors, bouncing it into a door, not realizing it was locked in place.

"Fuck. Pete, push on the other one, that one is locked."

"Why do they always lock the one on the right side—almost everybody is right-handed. Pisses me off."

Dixit jogged over and gave them an assist, pulling open the door on the left.

"Thanks Kev, this fucker is heavy!"

Rigor had set in and they carefully leaned the body against the wall of the building, catching their breaths.

Waxley and Golding joined them. Golding's jaw dropped.

"Well, this is verkakte. This is your deceased? Wrapped up in garbage bags and tape? Seriously? What the fuck, Kev?"

"Well, you know the M. E. can't be everywhere, especially on the cusp of a holiday, so sometimes we have to improvise."

Golding inhaled back mucus, producing a startling honking sound. He shook his head. "Yeah, that's some body bag."

There was a long pause.

He sighed. "Ok, let's get going."

• • •

September 21, 2015

Dinetta Laurence had never seen such teeth in a human face before. Winifred Singletary was greeting her, cheerily, but also with great compassion. She was communicating condolences for Laurence's great loss, but Laurence was completely absorbed in those teeth. The woman simply had the biggest teeth Laurence had ever seen—larger than any horse. And more plentiful, somehow. And her sympathetic head bobs were straight from a paddock. Dear Lord, put those things away...

"You were a close friend of Mrs. Elsrode?"

There was a pause. Laurence woke up.

"Well, no—actually, I'm a Detective. With the Police. We're... connecting with people who knew the deceased—you know, we sometimes find a helpful witness among family and friends."

She wanted to say that they were combing the scene for the murderer, but thought it wouldn't be appropriate at the victim's viewing.

"Yes, another policeman spoke with us just a few days ago, but I've forgotten his name, already. A very nice officer—sounded Jamaican?"

"Yes, that was Detective St. Bonaventure. He's meeting with a lot of persons who knew the Elsrodes." Laurence figured that was a nicer way of saying, 'he's interviewing and eliminating suspects.'

"It was shocking to us. Everyone loved Joyce. Who would want to hurt Joyce?"

The teeth receded back into the skull. Her face became solemn. She was on the verge of tears.

Just then, a smiling young man in a dark blue suit and oversized tortoise shell glasses swept in next to Winifred. He was wearing a deep green bow tie.

"Hi, I'm Bret, the Minister of Pastoral Care at Valley United Methodist. You've met my better half, Winnie? We were both dear friends of Philip and Joyce. This thing is unbelievable." He shook his head in disgust.

Laurence extended her hand. "Detective Dinetta Laurence. We're going to find the person that did this. They will be punished."

Shaking his hand, Laurence thought that at least this one had normal teeth.

"That's encouraging, Detective. These tragedies can shake our faith, but we must 'give ourselves to the Lord. If we trust in him, he will help us.'"

"Thanks Reverend Bret."

Laurence looked around the crowded room. The noise level was growing along with the general level of heat and discomfort. She saw Joyce's son, Jack Donnelly, speaking with Trimble. She spied Dixit chatting with an older man in clerical garb just to the side of the casket. She figured it was the Lead Pastor, William Weeks. Laurence had taken-on interviews with the victim's neighbors and current art students. St. Bonaventure and Quint had been assigned the 'church people.'

She was thinking that Dixit's suggestion to attend this viewing and to quietly photograph the attendees at the funeral, tomorrow, was more 'old school' bullshit. They had already worked through this entire group. Did a mystery killer really dare turn up at these things? It was a waste of valuable time.

She had not generated any suspects from her group. The victim's crop of 'students' consisted of a married couple and their grandchild. Besides alibiing one another, the grandparents lived in an 'over 55' gated community. All comings and goings were logged. They were nowhere near the victim on the evening of September 12th through the morning of the 13th. The grandson, age ten, was home with his parents. He was tucked away safely in bed. She had spent more time clearing the neighbors—seven homes on the cul-de-sac. A few neighbors had imperfect alibis— spouses alibiing each other—but none of those had any apparent connection to the victim other than geography and being normal, friendly neighbors. The neighbors were effectively eliminated.

Things were not looking good. It was approaching a week

now and the pressure to close the case was beyond intense. She had not been sleeping and home life had become a complete cluster for James and little 'Cil. She had an idea she would run by Dixit. There was an unfinished child's portrait found among the paintings. The 'art students' had not been involved in portraiture, so there was likely a recent customer for the unfinished work. She would pull a photo and have Bonaventure run it by the church people to see if they could identify the child. And then, as if on cue, she saw the very same kid waltz through the entrance of the funeral home with her parents. Surprise. She would introduce herself and get contact information for a later set of proper interviews—unless Bonaventure had already covered it.

Dixit was trying to find a way to unglue himself from the Reverend William Weeks. The old goat was not a suspect, but Dixit knew that informal chats often led to unexpected surprises. Today's "surprise" was being subjected to a theological discourse on Moses' "declination of admission into the Promised Land." Dixit had never heard an actual person use the word 'declination' spoken in a sentence. It got worse from there and Dixit found himself tuning-out. He roused himself somewhere around the discussion of 'Divine Assurance.' Was he a believer?

"Yes, I believe so."

There was a pause. Weeks was not fully satisfied by the response. It seemed equivocal. Yet it did indicate belief. Weeks was about to delve further into the ambiguity of the response, but then the Detective thanked him, shook his hand warmly and told him he had to move along to speak with his partner. Weeks was left to his own thoughts, as usual. And looking upon the gathered group of mourners—mostly his congregants—his eyes fell upon Singletary and his annoying wife.

Why had they been brought in two years ago? He had been

handling things perfectly well at Valley. Attendance was solid. Ok, it had improved a bit once these two, 'new young things' had come in and Singletary had taken over Pastoral Care. But he simply did not like Singletary. Those ridiculous 'trademark' silly bowties, worn constantly. And of every color and design imaginable. The female congregants loved to 'mother' him—sending him bowtie gifts as souvenirs from all over God's Creation. His always cheery and positive demeanor was downright annoying. Where was there room for the necessary solemn reflection and examination of conscience in a personality like that?

He sighed to himself. And that dreadful spouse with that frightening smile. How does a human skull hold so many teeth? She was just as annoying. And was it fair that the manuscripts over which he slaved were essentially ignored now and no longer publishable? No. And that Singletary's vapid prose would be published and successful was just too much to bear. Sure, "I Am Down With the Holy Spirit," was a clever 'contemporary' title for an otherwise 'feel-good' and decidedly un-Methodist Christian publication. But, why didn't his own publisher appreciate his 'dumbed-down' title for his most recent work, "What's Up, Nietzche? Signed, God." It was perfect—like that funny bumper sticker—just the sort of thing to bring out the college youngsters. But, no. Now he was now resigned to the dismal world of 'self-publishing'—first cousin to 'self-abuse' in his opinion. He chuckled to himself over the wordplay.

And woe to the sinner who played that extremely un-Christian practical joke on him. In an effort to spread the Word, it occurred to him that he could leave a spare copy of his book on the passenger seat of his car—and then leave all the doors unlocked! The thief would swoop up the book and perhaps get himself or herself saved through an otherwise sinful act. He hadn't had any takers, yet, but then one morning he went out to find that a second copy had joined his copy on the seat! One of the ungrateful congregants on whom he had bestowed a free copy had cruelly returned the book! Probably Singletary. He shook his head in disgust, but quickly came to attention when Singletary began addressing the group for an impromptu prayer and a short homily. He didn't mind. He had snagged the bigger fish—the funeral service tomorrow. Speaking from an elevated pulpit was always preferred to these 'campfire' talks.

"Friends, we face a sad parting. One of our Lord's lambs has returned to His flock, safe from the harsh realities of this mortal life. Our Joyce has now joined her Philip safely within the bosom of our Lord. For this we must be thankful and grateful. And I know this is a most difficult thing for us to understand. How does a merciful God allow this kind of tragedy in his Divine order? But this is not necessarily for us to understand. Remember God's response to the suffering Job? Have any of us called-up the morning and caused the dawn to know its place? Have we walked in the recesses of the deepest seas? No. We are humans. We can't do everything. We can't understand everything. Some things we simply must leave to God."

Singletary looked around and saw that he was getting through. Several faces had begun to tear-up.

"Now, how do we accomplish this impossible task of leaving this tragedy in God's hands? We use our faith. It is that simple. Faith. Do you remember Peter? He saw our Lord walking on water. He couldn't believe his eyes. He said, 'if that's you, Lord, tell me to join you out there.' And Jesus said 'yes—come on!' And there was Peter, believing that he could walk on water too. And guess what—he did! But then what happened? The minute it got a little windy and the sea a little rougher, he became afraid and lost faith! He began to sink like a stone. Jesus saved him, of course, but left us with a memorable Scriptural quote, 'Oh ye of little faith. Why did you doubt?' So, you see, if we all just believe that God's will is part of His Divine plan and must be done— even if we can't understand it—we can get through this. We will survive this—if we have faith. If we believe."

• • •

September 24, 2015

Over a week had passed and the case was officially cold. New murders were occupying the Detectives' time. The City's homicide assembly line churned forward, efficiently and relentlessly. At 5:45 AM, Dixit and Laurence were hunched over the conference table—the only ones in the bullpen. Dixit was rubbing his face. Laurence looked at the bruised bags under Dixit's eyes and wondered if hers looked as bad.

"We are missing something here, Detective. What have we missed?" Laurence didn't answer, sensing the question was rhetorical. Dixit continued. "I keep going back to that phone. Did we miss something?"

Laurence answered this time. "I can't see what? I triplechecked the call log, emails, texts against the server. There was nothing wiped."

"What else—web history? Photos?"

"I've checked the web surfing multiple times—nothing unusual, no web history deleted. And the photos are just pictures of her canvases. No painting had anything that would identify anyone—except the one, unfinished portrait of the kid, and we've eliminated those people."

Dixit stared off at the cubicle wall behind her, thinking. The bright lights of the halogen lamps caused him to blink, so he looked back down at his folded hands. Laurence gave him space. He looked up.

"Did you cross-check each photo with the photos on the server?"

Laurence looked on blankly.

"Not specifically. But I reviewed every image from the server and eliminated all the photos as having any evidential value—except the one of the kid. But I can cross check the phone images against the server, asap, sure."

She was thinking it was another waste of time like photographing the mourners at the funeral, which laid a complete goose egg.

"Yes please. I know we're clutching at straws, but let's be absolutely sure that no photo was wiped. We're fucking desperate here."

• • •

Dixit was in his assigned, unmarked car. This one didn't smell too bad, just stale smoke. Smoking was not permitted inside police vehicles, but oh well. He was driving over to the Admin. Building for another briefing. Thankfully, this was about departmental expenditures, not cases, especially the Elsrode case. He never thought he would see the day when he preferred a monthly expense briefing over a case briefing, especially this case. Boyce had become an off the charts pain in his ass. The pressure had become unbearable.

He was getting hungry and he knew there would be food there. The bean counters believed in comfort. He was organizing his thoughts when his cell jingled.

"Kev. I think I fucked up again."

He shriveled inwardly. He quickly spied the traffic in front and behind. He made a quick lane change and abruptly weaved his way over to the curb on East Fayette to concentrate. He heard the usual cacophony of car horns blast past him. No car was physically damaged in the maneuver. But one would have thought the world was ending based on the horn blasts.

"Ok Dinetta, let's not jump to conclusions. Walk me through."

"I should have crossed checked them all. I just didn't see the need."

"The photos? What did you find?"

"There's one photo on the server that was not on the phone. It's an abstract. It's hard to see exactly because the images produced from the server are kind of raw—you know, they do low resolution just to get the stuff off-loaded quickly for us. We can get a better resolution from them."

"Ok yes, they can do that. What was on the painting?" He was thinking that he should have asked, 'what is the painting?'

"It's weird. It's a woman's hand holding like a spatula or pancake turner—some kind of kitchen utensil—over a table. There's like a little tiny ball or something on the table underneath the hand and utensil. But there's no stove. Weird."

"That's it?"

"Yes. Very weird looking. The hand is very graceful."

"Ok. Email me a copy of it and then get the phone company to send us a high res. shot asap."

Dixit paused for a second, thinking. "I don't remember seeing a canvas like that — do you?"

"No. But there may have been. There were an awful lot there."

"Ok, get over to the crime scene asap and see if you can find that canvas. I'm guessing it won't be there. I'm hoping it won't be there because we need a break. If they wiped it from the phone, they would have removed it from the scene."

"Got it, Kev."

Dixit was still clutching the wheel even though he had stopped and pulled over. "Shit. Quint has the file and probably our copy of the key. And I know she's stuck in a trial today. Ok. Call the housekeeper and ask her to meet you there."

"Ok."

There was a pause and Laurence thought her cell had died. She looked at her phone to check the bars. Then she heard Kev's voice.

"No wait—better, just pull that key out of evidence. You know, the one you bagged from under the rock in the garden— the hidden key?"

"Yes."

"Forensics will have already lifted prints so they should let you have it. If it's a problem, tell them to text me so I can authorize release. That will be quicker. And you'll need to get it logged back in immediately after."

Laurence was thinking, 'yeah Kev. I know about chain of custody' but she kept her thoughts to herself.

"Got it, Kev."

• • •

By the time he had parked, Laurence had emailed the image. He expanded the image on his phone and scrolled around trying to figure it out. It was just as weird as Laurence had said. A lady's hand holding a utensil of some sort. There was a small thing on the table below the hand but the image became too blurry upon amplification.

Inside the Admin. Building, he snagged two croissants in a paper napkin and a coffee before being seated. He sat through a boring presentation by one of the financial officers. He did not care. He was barely listening with one ear and was thinking about the painting.

Within a few minutes, his phone began to vibrate. He saw it was Laurence and got up to take the call. None of the other attendees took particular notice. Cops jumping up to take calls were a common phenomenon.

"Kev, you're not going to believe this."

Dixit never liked the sound of that phrase. He paused to let Laurence continue.

"I'm here at the art studio. The key doesn't work."

"What do you mean the key doesn't work—what, the key you put into evidence?"

"Yes, it's the key I bagged from under the rock, but it doesn't work. I've tried it every possible way. It does not unlock that door."

• • •

Dixit was able to exit the budget meeting at the lunch break to meet Laurence back at the station. She had retrieved a higher resolution photo of the image from the phone company. She was sitting at her laptop while Dixit stood behind her looking at the image. Dixit was thinking that the higher resolution only made it look weirder.

"Kev, you know, that's a fly swatter the hand is holding."

"Yes, you're right. Wow. Scroll down."

Laurence did.

Dixit laughed. "Well, I guess we have our killer."

"Damn, Kev. I would have never thought."

Laurence had enlarged the image of the round thing below the flyswatter. It was a tiny housefly with enormous glasses smiling broadly and wearing a clownish bowtie.

• • •

They had spent the rest of the afternoon huddled in the bullpen getting their ducks in a row for the arrest. But there was a loose end.

"Why the hell didn't that key work?"

"Well, I spoke with Mrs. Espinosa and she said the key always worked. She wasn't sure why it wouldn't now."

Dixit was staring down at a print of the canvas. He was thinking about the wiped phone.

Laurence was looking off into space. Then her eyes lit up.

And then it hit Dixit. He had it. He looked over to see that Laurence already had it. He could tell by the gleam in her eyes.

"Kev! I think I know what happened!"

"Me too, Dinetta."

Dixit was at once proud and pleased for his mentee. But he couldn't help feeling a tiny twinge of jealousy. He knew that she had 'gotten it' perhaps a second or two before he did. He sighed to himself and thought perhaps he had lost a half step? Maybe. But he was still damned proud of Laurence and the work they'd done.

• • •

November 21, 1996

Ricciti thought he heard the sounds of Willoughby's footsteps padding down the office hallway. He heard him going into Tex's office.

Ricciti found Palanzo, elbow deep in files in his office.

"He's here. Let's read him the riot act."

"Are you sure, Lou? I mean he's just going to do whatever he wants to, right?"

"Fuck yeah Pete. I'm sure. I'm calling him out. He's fucking with our livelihoods—our lives—I won't take that shit."

Pete had not told Lou about the things he saw the night before. He couldn't bring himself to do it. He would at some point. Just not now. That morning, Lou had told him about the calls from the insurance companies. Pete felt sick, again.

Tex's office door was open. Willoughby was sitting at the desk sipping a beer and playing a video game on Tex's computer. His hand was a little shaky on the joystick. And his heart always raced a lot after his shot. Even after the workout. The guy at the gym told him it could happen, but developing bigger muscles was worth it. A cold beer from Tex's mini fridge always chilled him out. He would get over it. Too bad about Tex, though. He'd have to stock the fridge himself, now.

Lou spoke first: "Hey pal, we got a problem."

Willoughby did not look up from his game. "Problem, Shitty?"

Finally, he paused the game and looked up. "Oh, it's Shitty and Lasagna! How's your day goin' dagos?"

He laughed loudly, causing the snake on his neck to vibrate.

"Oh, you're a funny guy, Willoughby. You know, you smell like a fuckin' sewer rat. You might want to take a shower once in a while. But we're not here to discuss your lack of hygiene, asshole. We're here to tell you that we know what you're up to. We know you're burning down your piece of shit houses for insurance. And you are fucking stopping that right now, buddy!"

"Oh, I am?" He unpaused and went back to his game.

"Yeah, dickhead. We've had two calls this week from two different insurance companies about the claims filed by Mr. 'William Wilson.' Did you know he's using this office as his head-quarters? Hey, Mr. Wilson, did you know arson is a crime?"

"Only if you get caught, numb nuts. I've got a guy. It won't happen. Go back to sucking each other off and leave me the fuck alone or you'll regret it."

"Oh, you got a guy? What guy? We don't have a guy."

"Too bad for you. I do, fuckhead. A cop. So, I don't have any arsons. You better hope you don't either."

Ricciti was getting red in the face. "Listen you piece of shit, you are not burning down any more houses. Is that clear? Your Mr. Otto Chalk would not want to learn about your fucking him over for fire insurance money, would he? You are ending that shit, now!"

Willoughby paused the game again and breathed in deeply, several times. "I know where you live."

Ricciti looked over at Palanzo, quizzically, for support. But Palanzo was looking down at his shoes.

"What the fuck that's supposed to mean?"

"What do you think, genius? You have officially fucked with me. I will now fuck with you. Live and learn."

• • •

March, 1998

The three were sitting in the 'lounge' area of the Berninci Funeral Home in Essex. The chairs were padded aluminum. Foam rubber had been seeping through cracks of the vinyl seat cushions but the seats had been carefully attended to with grey duct tape. The table was Formica and aluminum, circa 1962. Coffee was available from beige machine for 25 cents. Two of the three had taken the plunge and each had received a lukewarm cup in return. Dixit's cup with artificial creamer and sugar was slightly more tepid than Chris' acidic black coffee.

Whitson was only 27 years old. None of them knew he was

a hemophiliac. Whitson seemed completely normal at Ignatius. He had no enemies but maybe no close friends. But they all liked him. They just didn't know Whitson all that well. But he was one of their cafeteria table guys, so Dixit, Golding and Waxley had made it to the viewing, in Essex.

"So, I might have to take a call from my agent—well, he's more of a bud than an actual agent, and there's no formal arrangement—but listen to this: there's a musical with a great part that I am up for and if I get the gig, I'll be at Center Stage! And some of those go 'off Broadway.' Woo hoo! 'Local boy makes good.' So, I may have to jump up and take a call..."

He didn't want to tell them it was a remake of "Annie."

Kev looked on approvingly. "That's great Chris. You bet!"

The Troll simply cast his eyes down towards his folded hands on the table. He involuntarily shook his head sideways and back again.

Waxley noticed but was unfazed. He took a sip of his coffee.

"Ok—here's a riddle for you guys!"

Waxley figured he would try to cheer everyone up. He, personally, did not want to think about Whitson. It was too fucking sad.

Golding and Dixit looked up, tiredly. Chris continued.

"I am a time traveler—but I can only travel forwards in time, not backwards! Who am I?"

Just then they all heard Waxley's cell ringing in his pants pocket. He pulled the phone out of his pocket dramatically and glanced at the screen.

"Shit—that's my guy. I've got to take this. Be right back!" Waxley headed from the 'lounge' and into the adjacent men's room.

Golding shook his head. "That's our boy, Kev. Off to see

Peter Pan and Tinkerbell. You know, he lives up here." Golding poked at his own noggin with his forefinger. "This place—upstairs. It's all upstairs."

"Well, he's got dreams, at least. Not everybody does."

Golding had stopped jabbing his head and went back to scowling.

"So, Brian—did you know Tim that well?"

Golding paused, thinking about it. "No, not really. Did you?"

"No, but I didn't think we needed to. He was completely a regular guy."

And that fast, Waxley came bounding out the door of the men's room, looking enthused and invigorated.

The Troll responded. "So, what's the answer?"

"Well, my guy said that they had closed the auditions, but to hang tight because a lot of guys wash out early on and then they look and grab the local talent. So, if that happens, my guy says that I'm well in the running!"

"Sounds promising, Chris!"

"Thanks, Kev!"

The Troll ignored the commentary, shaking his head. "Ok, great—but what's the answer?"

Waxley looked puzzled. "The answer? For me that means more rehearsal—which is cool, because I love to sing."

"No. To the riddle, Waxley." The Troll was scowling again.

"Oh, sorry Troll. Yes, the answer is "I am everyone.""

• • •

November 27, 1996

Intervening in some business dispute between Ricciti, Palanzo, and some other nut job was the last thing he wanted. It was the Wednesday afternoon before Thanksgiving. Everyone was getting out of Dodge. When the call came in from Palanzo earlier in the day, Dixit was thinking, 'couldn't they just put this business shit away and enjoy Thanksgiving?' And then in the system he saw there was a sheet on 'Willoughby,' alias 'Williams,' alias 'Waterstone,' alias 'Walters,' and a few others. It took a while to track down the actual jacket because it wasn't signed out. One of the guys in CID had it for some reason and it was buried deeply under piles on his desk.

He scowled to himself. A convicted pedophile last working Harrisburg, P.A., now gracing Baltimore with his presence. Wonderful. He was thinking how in God's name could those two idiots get involved with a child molester as a business partner? And then there were earlier assault convictions that sent the guy to prison twice beginning at the age of 19. And the multiple arrests for disorderly conduct, animal cruelty, arson, assault and battery, assault with a deadly weapon and even a homicide—one that apparently was never charged. But, approaching 3 PM, the day before the holiday—he really didn't want to know. He would go through the motions. He would help them make peace. And he would later let the two know that they were dealing with a twisted and very dangerous man.

A few loose sheets of notes and a bar napkin began sliding out of the file. He looked them over and then quickly pushed them back in. He tucked the jacket back into the pile on the desk.

• • •

Dixit had locked his firearm in the trunk of the patrol car. He didn't think he would need it and he didn't want the presence of a deadly weapon to incite the passions of a possible psychopath. He hoped he wouldn't regret the decision. And this would be quick. The trip up to the fifth floor on the office elevator was taking forever. He was composing his thoughts, trying to get himself in a peace-making frame of mind. Along with the clanking sound of the ancient elevator he thought he heard a car backfire in the distance. He listened. Just one. Yes, he had heard it. He was praying to God that it was a backfire from outside and not a gunshot.

The elevator door opened. Dixit didn't need to figure out the location of the meeting. He heard Ricciti's voice barking from one of the offices down the hall. Another voice was arguing back, loudly. As he approached the sound, he heard Ricciti screaming at the other voice, 'Are you out of your fucking mind?'

• • •

April, 1999

Dixit never liked eating lunch at 11 AM, but he didn't have much choice.

The bartender saw Hayman wander in. He didn't know the other guy. He wondered why Hayman would bring this guy into his bar? And this was damned early, even for Hayman.

The barman didn't say a word. He went to the tap and slowly poured out a pint of Pabst. Hayman took it away and headed to a table in the back. Dixit looked around.

"May I have a Coke, please?"

The bartender scowled and pulled a tiny half-pint glass from the slopwater in the sink. He dried the glass off, cursorily, with his damp, stained bar towel.

He held the glass to the tap and filled the glass with mostly soda fizz. He placed the glass down, sharply, on the bar counter.

"That's two bucks."

Dixit looked at the unappealing tiny glass of warm, brown fizz. He spied the little ashtray sitting at the corner of the bar. The worn sign said "Leave a penny. Take a penny."

116

He grabbed all of the change out of the ashtray. It looked about 32 cents.

"Here you go, sir. I think this will cover it."

He slapped the change onto the bar counter with the full force of his hand. The barman was temporarily awakened by the sound—the loudest so far of his day. Multiple coins rolled and plinked onto the floor. Dixit walked away leaving the glass of foam behind.

Hayman watched and shook his head as Dixit took a seat at the table. The tabletop wobbled, annoyingly.

"It doesn't do any good, Dixie. Jimmy's a fuckin' Pollack. You know, dumb as shit. He hates Blacks. He pretty much hates cops, too, but we go back."

Once Dixit got past the wobble of the tabletop, Hayman's words sunk in: to Hayman and his barman, he was "Black." He chucked, aloud.

"What's so funny?"

"Nothing Chief, nothing—another day, another two dollars."

Hayman shrugged. "Right. That's what I say. Who the fuck cares? I don't. I was raised to be open-minded when it came to minorities. You know, my dad used to say: 'Stanislof, there are good Blacks and bad Blacks. You can't judge them all the same.' And those are the words I live by. I am color blind when it comes to Black people. Good, decent, clean-living Black people are just as good as any white people."

Dixit was barely listening. It had never before occurred to him—and it shocked him. To some people, he was essentially 'Black'—a 'minority.' The revelation was bracing. Unbelievable. And then he remembered what Officer Melody Jurgen had said to him when he first went into the CID. She had asked, "Aren't you proud of the stance that the Department has taken on minority promotions?"

He had said, 'you mean Sergeant Al Sansbury?'

And she had said—'yes, him too.'

And all this time, people like Jurgen thought he was a minority. He couldn't believe it. Hilarious.

He noticed that Hayman was speaking to him.

"Hey, wake up, asshole. I think they're making nice."

He looked up to see the heavily tattooed barmaid, Leslie. She placed a fresh, large, icy Coca Cola in a Styrofoam cup before him.

"On the house, Officer. No hard feelings. Jimmy's a little hung over and grouchy."

Dixit looked over to the bar and gave a 'thumbs up' to the barman who begrudgingly, waved back. Dixit quickly fished a dollar from his wallet and handed it to the retreating barmaid, who thanked him.

Hayman nodded. "Jimmy's an ok guy. I told you."

• • •

November 25, 1996

Monday was the usual avalanche of kids, bus stop and supermarket. Now the Amway stuff was staring back at her in the face. She was wondering whether it was worth it. Lou kept telling her to drop it. She had lined-up a few customers but it seemed like it would take an awful long time before she'd see any real money. And it was fucking embarrassing asking her friends and then her family to get on board. And now she was begging from people she barely knew in high school. It kind of sucked.

Tracy came in from the backyard.

"Mommy, there's a funny looking man out there with Dom and Boh! He said he was our uncle but I don't think so. He said

Daddy was being bad at work!"

She looked out the kitchen window and was startled. Who the hell was that weird man in her back yard playing with her kid and her dog? He was sitting at their wooden picnic table looking over towards her, now, smiling. He stopped petting Boh and began rubbing Dom's head, as though he were a dog, too.

She slammed open the back screen door to the yard: "Get off my kid and my dog! Get the hell out of my yard!"

The man just smiled and ignored her. He waved a friendly wave and was now petting both Boh and her kid. She was nearly in shock.

"Dom! Get in here, right now!"

The boy moved away, cautiously, from the man and confusedly made his way towards his mother. Now the man was feeding treats to the dog, still petting the dog.

"I said get the hell out of here or I call the cops!"

The man stood and waved again. She saw the weird, wiry tattoo on his neck.

"Hi Patsy! I'm your Uncle Billy!" He was smiling again.

She yelled back: "We don't have an Uncle Billy, so I suggest you get the hell out of here, now!"

She felt flustered having to argue with the strange and frightening man. How did he know her name?

Dom had made it back inside the house.

"Tracy, sweetie, take Dom upstairs and wait there!"

She turned back and the man was again feeding treats to Boh. She grabbed her cordless phone.

"Mister, I don't know what you want, but get the hell out of here now! I'm calling 9-1-1!"

He laughed and walked to within ten yards of her.

"I'm your Uncle Billy. I work with Lou!"

"I don't care who the hell you are, get out of here!"

He laughed again.

"You should care! Listen, Louie has not been playing nice with Uncle Billy. Louie has done bad things and should let Uncle Billy take care of business so that Louie doesn't get hurt."

She noticed that Boh was now laying down near the picnic bench. That was weird.

"What are you talking about?"

"Well, let's just say that there are consequences for bad behavior. Louie wants to fuck Uncle Billy over, so… Gosh! What to do? Just let Lou know that Uncle Billy dropped by to say hello. That's all. Just a friendly chat."

The strange man was still smiling, broadly. Boh's body was now convulsing—foam formed at the dog's mouth.

"What did you do to my dog! Boh! Boh!"

"Have a nice afternoon, Patsy. Uncle Billy's leaving now, but I'll see you and the kids again, soon—real soon! Bye bye, Boh!"

The man then casually walked through the back yard gate to his car parked in the alley and drove away.

Patsy's hands and arms were shaking with fear. As soon as the man left, she ran out the back door to check on Boh. The dog was dead.

• • •

September 29, 2015

Dixit needed the cooperation of Lead Pastor William Weeks. It would be simple—just a couple minutes with the old buzzard to get the seed planted. He had the fancy law firm envelope with Trimble's authorization letter firmly planted in his breast pocket. He moved his hand inside his blazer and tapped his pocket making sure the envelope was still there. It was.

He was seated in the waiting area just outside the Pastor's office at Valley Methodist. The receptionist, stationed a few yards away, had phoned-in to let Pastor Weeks know that Detective Dixit had arrived for his meeting. But somehow Weeks would not open his damn office door and let him in. Instead, Dixit was treated to a wholly uninvited eavesdrop of a mind-numbing monolog. Weeks was rehearsing his homily for the upcoming Sunday. Dixit heard several of the same lines being read, over and over, with different inflections. And then sometimes, just the beginnings of sentences would be recited and then parts of sentences, followed by silence. And then the same sentence changed slightly with a different cadence and emphasis on certain words. And he could hear it all plain as day, because the Pastor was damn near yelling his guts out at his office wall.

It was all about the 'widow's mite.' How Jesus told his disciples that when the wealthy gave from their excess, there was no sacrifice at all. The real sacrifice came from the widow whose tiny offering represented everything she had. Weeks was saying her sacrifice made a difference. The rest did not. Theirs was for 'show.'

It took him back to third grade at St. Bart's. Sister Letitia Carpentia was beating the message into their young brains. Unless you gave 'til it hurts,' it was not real giving. How would giving someone your measly loose change gain you any indulgences? It would not. What kind of sacrifice would that be? If you didn't give your entire allowance to the poor—well, don't even bother giving anything. It would be a waste!

It had puzzled him and he raised his hand and asked, "but wouldn't the poor be glad to get at least something, instead of nothing?"

The insolence infuriated Sister Letitia and he quickly found himself alone sitting outside the Principal's Office—the frightening Sister Joachim—waiting for his punishment.

The Sister Principal opened her office door with a flourish. He felt a near vortex as the opening door sucked back the air near him, creating a vacuum. He was ushered inside and instructed to take a seat on the hard bench aside Sister's office wall.

Sister sat behind her desk and sternly glared over her reading glasses at him. She stared some more.

"Kev Dixit? It's Kevin, though, right? Kevin Dixit?"

He hated to correct Sister. "No Sister. It's just Kev."

He didn't want to tell her that his parents originally named him 'Kiev' and then legally changed his name to 'Kev' before he started grade school. His sister Constance had been 'Constantinople.'

She stared some more. And then she barked: "Dixit—cut the crap!"

That was it. She gave him a piece of penny candy from her jar and sent him back to class.

And then, finally, Pastor Weeks opened his door. "Ah, Officer Dixit, please come in!" He was going to correct him that he was "Detective" Dixit, but decided not to.

"Pastor Weeks, thanks for making time for me."

The two shook hands, warmly.

"Here's the letter from Mr. Trimble, the estate's lawyer." Dixit handed it over and watched Weeks return to his desk, retrieving a letter opener from the top drawer. He surgically sliced open the envelope and read.

"Yes Officer, this is fine. It's all in order. Please let the attorney and the family members know that we appreciate their generosity."

"I will. Now, to coordinate, could you give me some dates and times when you or someone on your staff would be available to pick-up the paintings you'd like? I can meet you over there."

"Yes, yes—I'll send Reverend Singletary. He's our 'outreach' minister. Let me check his calendar."

"Sure—mornings are best for me. I'm good this Thursday or Friday...."

Weeks went back to his phone and meticulously clicked the phone intercom button to ring his receptionist outside. Dixit was thinking he could have just stuck his head out the door and asked her.

"Mrs. Pyles, could you check Reverend Bret's appointments? Will he be free this Thursday or Friday morning?"

Dixit could hear her say: "Only this Thursday—10 AM."

Dixit spoke loudly to be heard outside the door, "works for me."

Pastor Weeks quickly held his hand over the mouthpiece and grimaced at Dixit's breach of protocol. He then responded into the handset, "yes, please enter an appointment for Reverend Bret for this Thursday at 10:00 AM for one hour. Have him see me when he gets in later today for instruction."

He replaced the handset firmly back into the cradle. Dixit was thinking that Weeks was one methodical Methodist.

"I would think an hour would give Reverend Singletary sufficient time to choose several of Mrs. Elsrode's paintings suitable for our annual flea market and bake sale."

"Yes—certainly. Bret can take as many as he likes—although a few of the canvases are unfinished."

"Yes, and I gather several are somewhat 'avant garde' in subject matter and hence not necessarily appropriate for our charity sale. Bret will be duly instructed."

"Of course."

"So, Officer, if you don't mind my asking, what's happened

in the case? You mentioned on the phone that the Police had concluded their investigation? Has there been an arrest?"

Dixit, looked down at his folded hands and scowled. "Well, please keep this confidential, but I'm afraid not, Pastor. Despite investigating every possible lead and every conceivable angle, we have concluded that Mrs. Elsrode was murdered by an unnamed and unidentified assailant—a person almost certainly unknown to the victim who, through some random circumstance, happened upon Mrs. Elsrode while she was working in her studio. Perhaps the assailant asked for money and Mrs. Elsrode refused to comply? We just don't know, but we feel pretty certain that this was a random crime and that the perpetrator is still on the loose."

Pastor Weeks shook his head, sympathetically sharing Dixit's frustration.

"These are troubling times Officer—very troubling."

"Yes. The only thing left for us to do is to wait for the assailant to make a mistake. Some of these people like to brag about their crimes. Word gets around. We get tips. Prosecutors reward defendants who come forward with tips that incriminate others. That's part of the system. We'll just sit back and wait. It's all we can do."

•••

Thursday October 1, 2015

Dixit, Laurence and the Reverend Bret Singletary had convened as planned outside the art studio of Joyce Elsrode. Laurence and Singletary had seated themselves on the sculpted cement bench along the pathway in front of the fish pond. Dixit was standing, impatiently glancing at his watch.

"I better give her a call. She's got the key."

Laurence and Singletary listened to Dixit's one way cell

conversation.

"Mrs. Espinosa? Yes, I'm fine, thanks. So, what's happened?"

There was a pause as Dixit nodded his head, listening.

"Oh, I'm sorry to hear that about Mr. Espinosa. Totally understand. Please send him our 'get wells.' Hey—would it be ok if I sent an officer over to your house to pick up the key?"

They saw Dixit listening and nodding. "Oh really? Ok—which one? Yes, hang on, let me check."

Dixit held his hand over the phone looked over at the garden and then spoke to Laurence and Singletary. "Mrs. Espinosa says she can't make it, but there's actually a key hidden under one of the garden rocks."

Dixit went back to his cell. "Ok—you say the oval one? The bigger one, about the size of coffee cup? Yes? Because there are a bunch of smaller ones... Yes? Good—hang on...."

He looked over to Singletary. "Reverend, look underneath that oval stone right there and see if there's a key there?"

He was pointing while holding his cell phone to his ear with his other hand. Singletary moved the stone and found the key. He held it up and gave a wan smile. "We've got it Mrs. Espinosa. Thanks, and, again, tell your husband we all hope he feels better."

He clicked off the cell.

"So Reverend, go ahead and do the honors. I'll hang back here and make a few more calls. Detective Laurence, give the Reverend a hand with whichever paintings he chooses."

Singletary approached the door with Laurence just behind. He looked at the key in his palm and said, "you know this thing looks kind of weathered—being out in the elements and all, it may not work—but let me give it a try."

He was beginning to sweat. He stuck the key into the door lock and gave two, quick, perfunctory turns, with no result. "How about that—I thought the key looked a little beaten up. It doesn't unlock the door."

Dixit put his cell aside. "Really? Detective Laurence—could you give it a try?"

Singletary handed the key over to Laurence. His hand was shaking. "Sure."

Laurence gave the key a simple turn and the door immediately opened.

Singletary looked stunned. Dixit put his phone away. "So, Reverend? What do you think of that? Why did the key work for us but not you? Because you knew it couldn't possibly work, right? You have to believe a key will work for it to work. That's just human nature. You didn't believe?"

"I... I..." he stammered.

Dixit was thinking, 'oh ye of little faith.'

"Ok, let's take a break while I tell you something important. You have the right to remain silent. Anything you say can and will be used against you in a court of law. You have the right to speak with an attorney before or during any questioning. If you cannot afford to hire an attorney, one will be appointed to represent you before any questioning, if you wish. You can decide at any time to exercise these rights and not answer any questions or make any statements. Do you understand each of these rights I have explained to you? Do you wish to talk to us now?"

Singletary had turned pale and looked faint.

"Did you understand what I said? Do you want me to repeat it for you?"

"Yes, yes. I understand. I get it." He sat back down on the concrete bench and put his face in his hands. He slowly shook his head, side to side, rubbing his hands over his face.

He looked up to Dixit and Laurence who were standing

126

above him. He took a breath.

"Ok, I can explain what happened and I think you will come to understand that it was a tragic accident. I would never hurt Joyce in a million years."

Laurence sat down next to Singletary and removed her note pad and pen. She began taking notes.

"So, yes, Joyce and I were lovers. Well, more or less. You see, when Philip was ill and in his home hospice situation, here, Joyce and I became close. I was their spiritual advisor and we do sometimes have the risk of our pastorate perhaps getting too close to us. It happens."

The color was coming back to his face and he was rallying.

"After Philip passed, Joyce and I continued to be close. I fell in love with her—deeply. I planned to leave Winifred and start a new life with Joyce. Joyce was sexy and artistic and cool. She had an easy laugh and a kind heart. I knew we were meant to be together, forever."

Laurence was writing notes furiously and had turned a third page in the tiny notebook.

"Now, whatever you do, Detectives—do not tell Winnie! She must never know. She would be crushed. And, besides, I resolved, internally, to make a new, fresh start with Winifred, after Joyce had died so tragically. So, Winifred must not know!"

Dixit blinked twice and looked over to Laurence who looked astonished.

"Well, Reverend, we can't make any promises about that—those things are out of our hands."

"Ok, ok, hopefully, I'll get a chance to explain all this to Winifred first...."

"Quite possibly. Now, just what happened that night, that Saturday, you must have gone over to see Joyce?"

"Yes, yes, we had consummated our love for one other once in a very passionate way just a few weeks before and I naturally sought more opportunities for intimacy with Joyce. More opportunities to demonstrate our spiritual bonding in a practical way, through the joy of our physical lovemaking."

'Horn dog,' Dixit thought.

"But despite my expressions of deep love for Joyce, she had grown cold. She had been putting me off—showing disinterest, notwithstanding the passion we had shared so completely."

He took a breath and placed his head back in his hands and crouched over. He looked up again, tearfully.

"So, yes that evening I made a surprise visit, as I was wont to do, now and then - but my Winnie believed I was out making Pastoral visits. Joyce of course let me into the studio."

He looked up. And gulped. The sleepy morning sun had evolved into a fierce midday laser. He felt the increased heat on his face. He shielded his eyes from the glare and spoke.

"So, she let me in, and it was not long before we were having a lovers' quarrel—a spat. I wanted her to commit to me, seriously and she... she did not. In fact, she laughed at me! I was shocked and hurt. I am a man, after all. I have my pride. And then while she was so giddily laughing at me and making fun of me, she revealed her latest canvas. It was her hand with a flyswatter about to cruelly strike at a small housefly, painted with glasses and a tie to represent me! Me! Well, in that moment of anger I did what any normal person would do. I defended my honor! I grabbed the closest paint knife from the stand and gave it a good swift shove! I don't know why I grabbed a paint knife, which can be dangerous, but defending myself with the knife felt like righteous indignation. But somehow, I must have struck at her too hard! I injured her! Badly. She immediately dropped to her knees and keeled over, knocking the canvas to the ground. She was lying there and I did everything I could do to help her. I looked around to find something to stop the bleeding, but it was too late. I could see that she had expired. I did say a silent prayer on her behalf, though."

This time Laurence looked over to Dixit in disbelief.

"So, Reverend, you accidently caused the death of Mrs. Elsrode. Why did you mess the place up? You must have taken the canvas?"

"Yes, yes. I know it sounds silly, but I thought it would be better for her family if it looked as though a stranger—a madman—had wandered in and taken her life in a rampage of some sort. Such would be easier for them to take than an accidental death at the hands of a true family friend and ally. You can understand that, right?"

"I understand what you are saying, yes."

"And, yes, I finished up and realized I need to get back on my evening schedule, so I took the shameful painting with me. Again, I did not want her family to see that side of Joyce—you know—her arrogance, her cruel streak...."

"Of course. But you came back? When did you come back?"

Singletary was sweating again. "Well, I had disposed of the painting in a dumpster at a grocery store a short drive from here and went home. But as soon as I got home to be with my Winnie, I remembered that Joyce always took photos of her paintings with her phone. At Valley, she would always show me what she had been working on. It gave her great joy. So, needless to say, I had a sleepless night. I needed to get over there and delete the photo of that canvas from her phone. Again, I wanted her memory to survive, unblemished. So, the next morning, I got myself ready for my Pastoral visits as early as possible without alerting suspicion.

Winnie just thought I was being an early bird that day. I got back to Joyce's just before sunup. Joyce had let me in before and the door was now locked, but luckily, I remembered the key hidden under the rock, so I let myself in and found her phone. I identified the photo and deleted it and then I left."

"Did you wipe down the phone when you were done, with a cloth?"

"Well, yes, I seem to recall doing so with my pocket kerchief."

"Ok, then what happened?"

"Well, I left and returned the key to the place under the stone. But when I got to the home of one of our flock for one of my scheduled weekly visits—it was Mrs. Hinton, because she is disabled and gave me her key so that she would not have to get over to the door for visits—the key didn't work. She had to let me in herself. It took me a minute to realize that I had left the wrong key under the rock!"

"Interesting."

"So, of course, after my visits were over, I did return to the studio that Sunday morning—well, actually, once I saw the Police involvement, I turned around and left. I never got the chance to exchange the key under the rock because the damn place was a crime scene. And I was very glad the other day when Pastor Weeks told me that you had called off the investigation, because I knew I would finally be able to get over here and exchange the key. I figured I would check things out today in connection with picking out the paintings. I'd see if the coast was clear for some time later."

He was scowling, now, still shading his face from the sun's glare.

"If that damned Mrs. Espinosa had gotten over here like she was supposed to, none of this would have happened."

Both Dixit and Laurence were trying not to smile. Singletary had so thoroughly bought into Dixit's fake call to Mrs. Espinosa. Singletary sighed and sat upright on the bench. "Well, Detectives, I have to say I do feel a lot better about this, having discussed it openly and candidly with you both."

Dixit responded: "Well, then, we are very happy that you feel better."

"I'm relieved that you both understand and are clearly not judgmental. I feel, deeply, that you both see how this was a tragic accident and how I had comported myself in a moral and just way, thereafter. I know that there will have to be some punishment meted out. That's how a just society works. I can picture significant community service as being appropriate. Accidents happen, but we all need to be more careful. A community service arrangement would be a 'win-win' for this community and for our congregants. I can picture myself interweaving my Pastoral work with the assigned community service. Broadening my spiritual outreach could help a lot of others whose lives are difficult or troubled. And, please Detective Dixit—let me break this to Pastor Weeks. He is elderly and it would be best to let me explain..."

Dixit looked over to Laurence in utter disbelief. Laurence was now smiling looking down at her notebook trying desperately to not let out a laugh.

"Well, Reverend Singletary, unfortunately, we are on the—shall we say—'acquisition' side of these investigative journeys. We... connect with and acquire and move the relevant person onto the next link in the chain, which will be the court system. The punishment phase is within the ambit of the court system, so Detective Laurence and I won't have any actual say in that. But, rest assured, the attorney you choose for this next part of your journey will definitely want to hear your views on community service, etc."

Dixit could barely control his facial expressions.

Singletary nodded, appreciatively.

"Now, Reverend, although this may seem unnecessary, I have to ask Detective Laurence to handcuff you and escort you to our car for safe transport on this next leg of your journey."

Singletary looked confused. "But wait—when did you want me to pick out the paintings for the flea market? Shall I do that first before you get me back to Valley?"

"No. That won't be necessary. We'll work on that later."

• • •

Dixit and Laurence were in the patrol car heading away from Central Booking back to the station. A sense of real peace was in the air. They could finally move this case off of their board.

"So, Kev—what if Singletary was able to open the door?" She was thinking that Dixit's plan was more old school detective bullshit.

"Well, we had him one way or the other. The key you took into evidence belonged to Mrs. Hinton and it's not like a wheel-chair-bound woman went out on a mission to first retrieve her key from Singletary and then plant it under a rock in the garden of a studio she had never visited. The circumstantial evidence would be overwhelming. But I figured we could plant the real key back under the rock and the whole 'key' thing would throw Singletary off his game and lead to a confession."

"Well Kev, I have to admit it did work."

"And did you catch the operation of that other old chestnut? 'The killer always returns to the scene of the crime?'"

He was smiling to himself. He knew his 'old school' stuff

annoyed the hell out of the younger cops like Laurence.

"Well, yes, there you go, Kev. He did return to the scene that morning, didn't he..." She grimaced to herself.

• • •

November 27, 1996

Palanzo stood in front of Ricciti's desk and watched Ricciti stretch out in his office chair. Ricciti was slowly rolling his chair forward and backward, tapping the wall behind and then pushing forward until his stomach touched the top desk drawer. Then he reached into the desk drawer and removed the .38 revolver. He gripped the pistol feeling its weight. He pulled the hammer back, just a bit and let it gently return. It looked ready.

"I should have never given that to you, Lou. If my dad were alive he would kill me if he knew I took it."

Palanzo was thinking back to the severe sermons his dad would preach about respecting the weapon and never letting it become your master. Yet, it was something his dad was forced to use in his younger days, when collecting slots money from the bars in Southern Maryland. He wasn't even sure it would work. It had been sitting in the canvas bag along with an ancient cardboard box of bullets at the bottom of his dad's workbench, covered with a handsaw and two massive wrenches. It hadn't been moved in over 30 years.

"Ok. It's almost 3 o'clock. Now, chill out, Pete. I've got this."

Palanzo looked down towards his feet.

"Lou—don't be pissed, I know we agreed. But I've been thinking—it's all I can think about—we can't do it, man. I can't. There's got to be some other way out of this. Not with a gun. You don't really want to kill the guy, right? We got to get some help."

"What are you saying Pete? Don't back out on me, now,

man! That piece of shit is on his way up here like we agreed and he's going to get the fuck out of town and away from my family or take a bullet in his maggot-filled heart! Look. We're going to give him an out. I'm going to ask him nicely to get the fuck out of Baltimore and never go near my wife and kids again. Do you think he'll go along with that, Pete? I don't know, but if he doesn't it will be on him, not us, ok? He killed my fuckin' dog, Pete. Ok?"

"Lou. I called Kev."

"What did you say? Our Kev? You called our Kev, who happens to be a cop? Are you out of your fuckin' mind, Pete? What did you tell him!"

Lou returned the pistol and brusquely slammed the top drawer.

"Jesus! I didn't tell him the whole thing—I just told him about Willoughby being a violent guy who was trying to intimidate us and take over our business. That he threatened us and your family. That we were meeting with him at 3 and if Kev could come by and act as a mediator or whatever it might help to scare Willoughby off."

"So does he know that fucking Willoughby murdered Tex and burned his body in an arson—of a building that we're not even sure was ours?"

Pete was about to tell Lou that he had not mentioned any of that but was startled to hear the sound of laughter. They both looked up to see Willoughby standing in the doorway.

"Well, congratulations, boys! I didn't think you knew about the little joke I played on Tex. But, you know, that Tex was really a bad man. He had it in for ole Billy—got himself a nice life insurance policy—on me that is. I found it on him a few days ago when we were playing patty cake together. He named himself the beneficiary, so he had to go bye-bye."

Ricciti, now panicked, scrambled to pull open the desk drawer. Willoughby took two quick paces and forcefully jammed the drawer back in place, crushing Ricciti's wrist between the drawer and desktop.

Ricciti stood instinctively, screaming in pain as the drawer bounced back open, exposing the revolver. Willoughby head-butted the screaming Ricciti and followed with a quick set of vicious body blows to his kidney. The snake on Willoughby's neck undulated with excitement. Willoughby then shoved Ricciti's crumpling body aside with both hands, tumbling him onto the floor next to the desk. Ricciti, on all fours, gasped for air as he clutched his wrist in anguish.

Willoughby calmly took the seat behind the desk and pulled out the gun. "Looky here!" He held the gun up examining it under the fluorescent office lights. "So that's what you were after! Whoda thunk!" He dangled the gun by the trigger guard and began twirling it around. "Sweet, very sweet. What a piece of shit!"

Ricciti was now barely standing, hunched over in pain, rubbing his wrist and side. Palanzo, in shock, had not moved an inch. Ricciti gamely moved closer to the desk, pointing to the gun. "Put that away asshole—that's ours!"

Willoughby stopped twirling the gun and held it menacingly on the two. "Really? Finders' keepers, dickhead. Now just step back there with your fellow wop, Shitty. I've got the gun now in case you didn't notice."

The two stood together facing the desk.

"Ya know, seeing you two guineas reminds me of a joke. Have you heard of them new Italian tires? When dago flat, dago wop, wop, wop! Dago wop, wop!" Willoughby began laughing hysterically. The snake tattoo writhed furiously as if trying to free itself from his neck. "You're not laughing?"

Willoughby pointed the gun at a place between their heads and pulled the trigger. The bullet whizzed past their skulls, missing Palanzo's right ear by inches. The deafening sound reverberated throughout the office suite. Palanzo immediately covered both ringing ears and fell to his knees stricken with nausea. Ricciti stood open-mouthed, in a state of shock. He quickly recovered.

"Are you insane!?" Ricciti's ears were ringing and he yelled again over the noise. "Are you fucking crazy?!"

Willoughby stared thoughtfully at the pistol and checked the cylinder, making sure the next round was loaded in the chamber. He saw his own hand twitch a little and remembered that he was going to beat the living shit out of that asshole at the gym who stocked him up with those fucked-up meds. He looked back up.

"No need to get excited, dago. Just wanted to see if your piece of shit worked. Looks like it did!"

He looked at the gun again, holding it out in his hand as though to offer it to Ricciti. Then he quickly withdrew the pistol.

"Never mind. I'll keep it!"

He palmed the gun from his right hand to left hand and back.

"You know, this old piece of shit is not too bad for a Saturday night special. I think I'll take another shot."

Ricciti screamed: "Are you out of your fucking mind!?"

"Me? No. But what about you? What the fuck did you think you were going to do, here? Run me off my stake? You two numb nuts have fucked up this operation completely and interfered with my side hustle—which is gonna cost you both!"

Just then Willoughby looked up from his desk seat and saw a uniformed policeman standing at the office doorway.

"What the fuck, Shitty? Did you call 5-0 on us?"

He stared Dixit up and down, pointing the gun directly at him. "You know, I bet you actually are Hawaiian? You look it! A real 5-0! Hey, book 'em Dano!" He began laughing menacingly, but his hand continued its tremor.

Dixit advanced through the doorway, holding his arms and hands out before him, signaling peaceful intentions. "It's cool man. All cool here. I just dropped by to see if I could help out the situation."

Willoughby continued to hold the gun on Dixit who took his place next to a now upright Palanzo.

"So, 5-0, just how much of that did you hear? How the fuck long have you been eavesdropping there?"

"Hey man, I just got here. It's cool. I don't know anything and no one has to know anything about that gun if you just hand it over. Then, we can all take a breath, chill out and discuss whatever problem is happening here, today, ok?"

Dixit was hoping like hell that the psycho would hand over the gun, but he wasn't going to put any money on it.

Willoughby looked at the three and then opened the cylinder of the gun, checking the bullet count. He closed the cylinder, sharply. "No, I think I'll hang on to ole' Smokey here. I like her."

"Ok, that's cool man. But how about just lowering it so we can all chill and talk this thing through?" He was nodding his head trying to get a conciliatory rhythm going in the room.

Willoughby trained the gun directly on Dixit. "No, sorry 5-0. Too late. This place is burned. All of you are going to go bye bye, now and you get to go first!"

Dixit was waving his hands instinctively, defensively trying to reign-in the madman.

Immediately he heard a shot—louder than he would have expected from a 38, almost like it had its own echo. He felt something whizz by his ear nicking his patrol cap, tipping it sideways on his head. He was still frantically motioning with his hands. Through the ringing in his head, he saw Willoughby writhing in his chair, blood soaking his firing hand and surging out of his jugular vein, the snake on his neck dancing rhythmically to the spurting blood. He saw blood splashed against the wall behind the desk.

Palanzo dropped to his knees and retched profusely into the office trashcan.

Ricciti stood motionless, mouth agape, repeating, "What the fuck... what the fuck... what the fuck..."

Willoughby was desperately trying to breathe, his body pulsing in agony, but every breath just pumped more blood out of the wound. The gun dropped from his bloodied hand onto the floor. The writing stopped and his body slumped over in the office chair.

Dixit saw motion peripherally and looked over towards the door frame. He saw the uniformed forearm and police-issued firearm pointing into the room. The hand was beginning to shake as smoke wafted lazily towards the ceiling from the end of the barrel.

"Kev—did I kill him? Did I kill the guy?"

He saw it was Jurgen. She was supposed to have stayed in the patrol car.

Dixit looked at the now dead Willoughby and instantaneously remembered the hardship he had faced for his first 'killing.' Stuck behind a desk with nothing to do for months; endless interviews with police superiors and the union; the attorneys; the endless hours with that first police shrink until he was finally cleared again for service thanks to Bhavna. All because of that guy with the butcher's knife straddling the woman lying on the sidewalk. He had relived it a million times. He had yelled at the guy to stop. He had identified himself as police. He had yelled to stop several more times. But the guy just kept plunging the butcher's knife in, again and again, deeper and deeper into the back of the prone body of the woman who was screaming in agony.

He had pulled his weapon and given the guy one more command to put the knife down. But the guy didn't and was about to plunge the knife in one more time when Dixit shot the man dead. The victim was medevac'd to Shock Trauma. After 11 surgeries, she somehow survived. Dixit and the Baltimore City Police Department were rewarded with a wrongful death lawsuit. Loss of consortium was painful and traumatic for the victim, more so than the stabbings. She loved her husband. The Police didn't understand his psychiatric problems. A favorable out of court settlement did not ease her existential pain, but at least gave her a platform on which to rail against Police wrongdoing.

Dixit was sweating, reliving the memory. He would not let that happen to Jurgen. "No, no Jurgen. You didn't kill him. Look at his hand. The gun misfired. His own bullet took a crazy angle up into his neck. Your slug went over there."

He was pointing to an imaginary place behind the desk. But there was no question that she had shot Willoughby in his firing hand with the bullet ricocheting off of the gun and into his jugular. Willoughby's point-blank shot at Dixit was deflected. He was thinking, had she not fired, he would be dead.

"Are you sure Kev? Really? I thought I might have killed him. I didn't want to. But...."

"No, no, Melody. I'm absolutely sure. Your bullet did not touch him."

"Oh, thank God, Kev. Thank God!"

She entered the office and looked at Palanzo crawling up and away from the stench-filled basket. She saw Ricciti, still standing, silently frozen but for the expanding area of urine saturating his pants leg.

"What happened here? I know you said to stay in the car, but I thought I heard a gunshot and came right up!"

"You did the right thing, Melody." Dixit stared over to a now wobbly Palanzo and thunderstruck Ricciti, to get their attention. "This unfortunate guy with the gun was likely some poor nut who showed up here with bad intentions. This happens you know. Psych cases go a little crazy during the holidays. These guys weren't expecting any of this."

The two kept their mouths shut.

"Shit Kev, this is really going to screw things up for me with Michael tonight. I'm supposed to meet him at his office in a few minutes and after dinner finally meet his kids. We're going to take them to the bonfire at school. Now we'll have to get the M. E. and Forensics in and this will be another all-nighter. Shit!"

Dixit shook his head. "No way, Jurgen—you put in for your time and you are going to get it. I can handle the mop-up and paperwork. You've been off-duty since 3. Just get on out of here and let me handle it. And have a great Thanksgiving!"

"Really?"

"Yes, really—get on out of here. That's an order!"

"Kev—I can't thank you enough for this! Michael—well, we're starting to get serious, and he's put up with so much of my scheduling shit..."

"It's ok, Melody."

"I'll leave the car for you. I was just going to walk over to Michael's office from here, anyway."

"That's fine, Melody."

She became suddenly crestfallen. "Crap. That's not going to work. I fired my service revolver in the line of duty and this guy's dead. Even though I didn't hit the guy, I have to take my weapon in and fill out the report and all that. Shit!"

Dixit did a quick mental calculation. "No—not actually. The regs only require the report if a service weapon is used in the course of a homicide. This guy was a suicide. His gun misfired. See? He actually killed himself."

"Oh, wow—yes, you're right Kev. Whew! Saved again!" She was almost out the door, but turned back to say: "And Happy Thanksgiving to you, too, Kev, and you other guys."

And then she was gone.

• • •

April, 1997

"Kev, I love you. You know that, right?"

Kev knew he was in trouble—or that a big 'ask' was on the way. He steeled himself.

"Yes, my lotus...."

"He has to go, Kev. I'm so sorry. But he has to go. It's time for the baby bird to fly from the nest again. It's time."

Dixit sighed to himself. This was going to be tough. "Well, yes. He does need to move on. And, you can see, his twelve-step has been working for him. He's totally embraced it. More than totally. He's just plain into it."

Bhavna scowled. "Yes, Kev. And that is really good. But he can be totally into his program from another place, right? He can't keep crashing here, over and over, forever. It's embarrassing."

"Why?"

"Why? I've told you 'why.' We always tell him that we can't offer him kitchen privileges—that he'd have to make do with the microwave and fridge we put in the garage... for him. That's always the condition. We have a child who we want to raise in a normal, healthy, environment. Why is Alan wandering around in the kitchen at various times during the day—usually in a bathrobe, and with nothing else underneath. The other day I found him looking through our fridge and his robe was open. He turned around and gave me a 'full frontal' view of his privates—all of them hanging all out. Thank God no one else was around. And why is he mooching from our fridge? It is galling, Kev. He is taking advantage of us."

Dixit knew everything she was saying was right. "I know. I know. He's always been a mess. He doesn't mean any harm. He's... eccentric."

"Well, that's nice for him. But what about Vadin? I've got my hands full running after him all day and Alan wanders in and out of our home at all hours distracting him. It's unsettling."

"But Vadin likes Alan? Alan is kind of like his adopted uncle?"

"Yes, that's great for Alan, but when I have to drag Vadin away, he doesn't like it. He pitches a fit and I become the 'bad guy.' Come on, Kev—I need you!"

He could see that the situation was really upsetting her. She might be crying. He went to her and held her, closely. "Bhavna, my Bhavna—I love you and will make this right. Everything you've said is right. He does need to move on. I am so sorry."

He began stroking her long black hair. "Tomorrow, Alan will be gone. I promise. Let me speak to him, now, and get him out of here by tomorrow."

· · ·

Dixit went out the front door of his home to the end of his driveway and rapped on his own garage door. There was no response. But he knew Alan had to be in there because he heard the sound of Kev's own mini-TV, borrowed by Switzer several weeks earlier. He rapped even louder.

Finally, he heard the voice of a groggy Alan Switzer, "hold your horses—I'm coming!"

The garage door raised and Dixit saw Switzer standing wearing only saggy underpants.

"Hey Kev! Good to see you! What brings you over?"

"Well, Alan—I came over to let you know about some really good news! But, feel free to toss on a robe or something so you don't catch cold!"

"You bet, Kev!" Switzer grabbed a thick, plaid comforter and held it around himself like a robe.

They both took aluminum lawn chairs that had been scattered around the garage and sat at the card table. As he was taking a seat, Dixit looked over to the cot. The mattress appeared to have a large moldy spot in the shape of a man. He quickly looked away.

"So, Kev! Let's hear the news!"

"Ok, Alan. Well, it is really clear that your twelve-step program has been working for you, so it's time for a new challenge!"

Dixit delivered the message in the same voice used to convince Vadin to eat his vegetables. He was hoping for different results with Switzer.

"Awesome, Kev! What's the challenge? What can I help you with? Is it investment advice—because if it is, I have been doing a lot of research and have a couple incredible leads for you!"

"Well not quite, Alan. But it does concern... 'asset allocation and... realignment.'"

"That's great Kev. Diversity in your portfolio is really the key! Look, let me tell you about this one thing—ok, it is a little risqué at the present time—but is guaranteed to be mainstream, very soon. If you get in on the ground floor, you will be golden!"

Dixit bit. "Yes?"

"Medicinal cannabis. Yes, that's right! So, as you know I've been riding your bike over to the program, 3 days a week—and you probably didn't know it—you guys have an incredible public library, right there. It's just a couple blocks away, so as soon as I'm done my work in the program, I just cycle down to the library and do investment research. They have computers there that can connect you to the world wide web through telephone modems. You sign-in and they give you twenty minutes at a time—just so one person doesn't hog the whole thing."

"Of course."

"And at that time of day, I'm usually the only person trying to use a computer with modem capability so, I wind-up staying there often for hours. And people haven't complained too much, either…"

"Interesting."

"So, anyway, that's where I read about new developments in cannabis that are being promoted by the medical field. A lot of big-name physicians and psychiatrists are now endorsing cannabis as a treatment for depression and other maladies, like malarial diseases."

"How about that."

"Yes, and I've read their studies—which I can comprehend, thanks to my medical background, and I believe there is something there. The medical cannabis industry has its own lobbyist in DC and will soon gain support from some of the big policy makers on the Hill. Marijuana will almost certainly be available, legally dispensed by medical doctors, probably within two years. Maybe sooner. It will certainly be decriminalized at the federal level within a year or so."

"Well, that's quite fascinating, Alan—but you know, I'm in

the cop's retirement plan at work, so that's where I sock my extra money. I'll get a pension from the City, but I also invest in their 401K plan—which is where my extra savings goes. They have some kind of mutual funds and things so that you don't get too tied-up in any one security. You know 'don't put all your eggs in one basket.'"

"Sure, Kev!" Switzer was not terribly surprised that Kev didn't 'get it.' He was kind of a fossil...

"But, Alan, let me get to the point. The exciting news is that it is time for us to cut you loose. We've been selfishly enjoying your company, but I think we all know, you've done a great job with your program and need to be free and independent again. We can't continue to impose."

'Yes,' Switzer thought—he hadn't wanted to complain, but babysitting Vadin and keeping everyone in good spirits was not an easy job for him. Maybe they had been taking advantage of him a little—but he would always let that slide because at heart, Kev was a good guy. He never let his people down.

"Kev—I hate to admit it, but I think you're correct. I'd been putting off this day for a long time. I didn't want to let you guys down. But, yes. Let me get my shit together and I'll be out of here in a week!"

• • •

"Ok, my lotus... So, progress has been made."

Bhavna did not like the sound of that. It meant that Switzer was almost certainly going to be in the garage, tomorrow. "Oh—progress, Kev?"

He could tell she sounded a little cold. "Well—we reached a compromise. He knows he has to get on out of here but asked for a week. So, I said, 'yes.' I know—not ideal—but it is a commitment and I promise you he will be out in a week. And if not, I will change the lock on the garage and I'll get him out. Ok?"

Bhavna could tell that Kev had done the best he could. She gave him a mild, 'Ok.' "What were you discussing in there, all that time? He had you in there for almost a half hour?"

Dixit chuckled and rolled his eyes. "Well, crazy investment ideas."

"Figures—from a man with no means."

"Here's one—'medicinal cannabis'—because the medical community has allies in Washington to decriminalize marijuana within a year."

Bhavna barked out a chuckle. "Good Lord—that's deranged—will never happen."

"Oh—the other one is even better. Listen to this: a store that you can't go to, but can only connect to by a phone modem from your computer."

Bhavna chuckled. "What does the store sell?"

"This is the funniest part: books. The store sells books!"

Bhavna broke into a loud laugh and Kev joined her. "Books? People go to bookstores and libraries. Who the heck would go to the trouble of hooking up their phone to a modem to shop on a computer—for books?"

"I don't know!"

"What is the store called?"

"Um—let me think, it was something about the rain forest—now I've forgotten—but Alan said you can buy the stock at a really good price now..."

• • •

They had gotten through the difficult day. Vadin was put to

bed and asleep now. They could be alone. He held her closely on the sofa in the living room. He caressed the side of her head. He kissed her forehead.

"Just what sort of hold does this strange man have over you?"

Dixit laughed. "He is one of my neighbor friends. They lived up the street from us. I grew up with them all. One of the kids, Clay, was in my class."

"But Alan was not your classmate?"

"No. He was a couple years older. But he went to Ignatius, too. He knew all of us guys because of his brother. He'd stop by and hang out with our table sometimes."

"Your table?"

"Well, that was like our 'clique.' We all hung out together at a certain table in the cafeteria. That's how we knew each other."

"A table? How did you form this 'clique?'"

"Well, we were freshmen and didn't know anybody and we all wound up eating at the same table in the cafeteria and became friends."

"So, you had nothing else in common but sitting at the same table?" 'Like a pack of dogs,' Bhvana thought.

"Well, we were all freshmen. We had that in common."

He didn't want to tell her that there were 'jock' tables and 'cool guy' tables and 'intellectual' tables and 'artistic' tables and 'nerd' tables. Theirs was kind of a 'none of the above' table.

• • •

November 27, 1996

"Ok, everybody—let's all just take a breath."

Dixit was looking over at Palanzo, who had vomited, and Ricciti, who had urinated himself. And, he didn't want to, but he found himself gazing over at the corpse slumped over in the office chair behind the desk. There were many problems here.

Ricciti was still trembling. "Kev, what the fuck are we supposed to do, now?"

Dixit looked around at the horror that used to be an ordinary office.

"Well, it looks like we need to get things back in order, here." Dixit was nodding his head as though he actually had an idea as to what the hell was going on.

Palanzo was finally becoming sentient. "Kev, did Willoughby really shoot himself?"

Ricciti jumped in: "Pete, dickhead—that's what Kev said, so that's obviously what happened. He's the Police, ok?"

"Ok, sorry Lou! It's just that a lot of shit here happened really quickly!"

They all became quiet.

Palanzo said: "You know, I think Willoughby's dead?"

Ricciti looked over to Palanzo in disbelief.

"Kev—we've got to get this guy out of here and dump him somewhere. We could go out Northpoint Boulevard—plenty of woods and shit up there...."

Dixit had been looking around at the chaos. He noticed his hands were trembling a little. He steeled himself.

"Lou. No. We've got to give the guy a burial."

"A burial—you mean like a real funeral? Are you shittin' me?"

"Well, a burial as a... means of disposal. We can't drop a human body into the woods. I am the Police, remember?"

"Ok."

Ricciti looked around again at the chaotic crime scene. He began shaking again. "Kev, our people will be coming back to work here after Thanksgiving—what the fuck are we supposed to do?"

"Ok, Lou—don't panic. Look, we've got the rest of today and Thanksgiving Day to get things back in order before your staff show up on Friday, right?"

Palanzo jumped in: "No, Kev. We gave the staff off for the day after Thanksgiving. I don't think anyone should be back here except for me and Lou before Monday."

Then Ricciti said: "Fuck—but we've got the usual cleaning people coming back in!"

"Yeah, but Lou, they won't be here tomorrow or Friday. They'll come on Saturday."

"Ok. Yeah."

Dixit spoke up: "Let's set a goal. We get this place back to normal and this guy properly buried by Friday night." Kev looked at his watch. "It's only about 3:30, now. We've got several hours today to get things started before we have to get out of here. How are you guys for tomorrow? Any availability?" He looked over at Ricciti.

"Thanksgiving Day? Shit, Kev. No. Patsy will need me all day. It's a whole big thing with the kids and her folks...."

"Ok. Pete?"

"Sorry Kev. I'm taking my mom out for Thanksgiving dinner and then I go over to my ex and pick-up my kids for a couple hours. That was in the settlement agreement."

"Ok Pete. But you guys are available Friday, right?"

Both nodded. Pete said, "yeah, all day."

"Ok. We'll get the basics done here in the next couple hours and then meet back here on Friday to wrap up things and... arrange the burial."

Ricciti looked horrified. "You mean leave this guy here until Friday? Like this?"

He was pointing to the bloodied corpse slumped over in the

chair. There was now a bad smell coming from that direction.

"Well, he stays here—but not like that. We'll get him in a...
body bag."

Dixit saw their puzzled looks.

"We'll make one."

"Kev, where do we begin?" Ricciti was holding out his arm,
as though displaying the chaos in the room for the first time to
Dixit.

"Ok. First, don't come near this guy now because you'll get
blood all over your clothes and shoes. We'll need some of those
green plastic trash bags. The largest size—the sturdiest you can
find. Several boxes. We'll make ponchos out of three of them and
use the rest for the body bag. And we'll need some rubber gloves.
You know—for dishwashing or surgical latex gloves—any kind
of glove like that. And we'll need duct tape or some other strong
wrapping tape." Dixit paused for a second, thinking. "And we'll
need some of those gallon size freezer bags—sturdy ones. We'll
put them over our shoes."

Palanzo chimed in: "Do you want the ones with the sliders or
the other kind?"

'Seriously?' Dixit thought.

"Pete, you know—it probably won't matter because we're
going to tape them closed over our feet."

"Ok Kev."

"And we'll need a bunch of rolls of paper towels—a couple of
large packages—you know, multiple rolls."

"Shit, Kev. We've got paper towels in the Men's room. Should
I just get those?"

Dixit was already shaking his head. "No, Lou. The less foot
traffic around here, the better."

Ricciti and Palanzo simply stared back at Dixit.

"Ok, one last thing—3 long sleeve sweat shirts. Anything with long sleeves to keep the blood off our arms."

Palanzo said, "what size, Kev?"

Ricciti thought, 'shit, this is getting expensive,' but he didn't dare verbalize his feelings.

"Size? Probably extra-large to fit over our clothes? Get the largest. But, whatever they have, we'll work with it."

Dixit was met with more blank stares. "Guys, you should be able to find that stuff at the drugstore around the corner—one of those CVS or Rite Aids? They usually have all that stuff." They both nodded.

Dixit looked forlornly at the scene and down towards the remains of the gun, lying on the floor below the desk.

"Did you guys know that this guy was carrying a gun?"

Lou looked over to Pete.

"No, Kev."

The room went quiet again. Dixit was staring ahead, concentrating.

"You know, we're going to need some extra help with this. Some more manpower. A couple more guys. Some to finish the mop-up here Friday, some to do the burial. We're going to need to replace parts of the carpet and repaint at least the one wall. That blood will never wash off the wall." He was pointing to the wall behind the desk.

Palanzo spoke up. "Kev, getting other people involved—is that such a good idea? How would we trust them?"

"Well, it would be our guys. You know, guys like Chris Waxley—who's up for anything—and Brian Golding—because he can handle the burial?"

Ricciti looked puzzled. The Troll? Yeah, well, he's probably still got that fucking hearse."

"Yes—but we've got to get these guys lined up, now. I'll phone them while you two get those things: big green trash bags, gloves, gallon bags, tape, sweatshirts and paper towels." He was counting off the items with his fingers as he spoke. He walked over closer to the dead body. "There's still a lot of blood seeping out of this guy. We'll need to try to tape down the wound area once you guys get back here."

• • •

Dixit was alone and was thinking about the logistics of the burial and dragging Golding into the mess. He was hoping it wouldn't be that much different than the last time he had reached-out to Brian for help. He opened his flip phone and dialed.

"Golding."

"Hey Brian—it's Kev. Happy almost Thanksgiving to you!"

"Hey Kev—you too. What's up? How you been?"

"Well—you know I've been great. Now, I don't like to impose on you, but I might need some help, again." Dixit was staring at the corpse.

The Troll mused and responded, cautiously. "Ok Kev—you got another dead one?"

"Well—yeah. Same kind of thing, basically. Remember the other old guy? Homeless with no one claiming him, but had the number tattooed on his wrist, so we figured he'd want a proper Jewish burial—not a cremation? This guy is... similar. Not so much any religious stuff but basically he wound up in a place where he didn't belong and died."

"Yeah, it's that time of the year when the homeless go anywhere but a shelter to stay warm and bad shit happens. It sucks."

"Yes, this was pretty sad. Do you think that cemetery could

152

find him a spot? He's not Jewish, I don't think?" He paused. "Probably non-denominational."

"Yeah, there's a section where they bury paupers and non-Jews and guys like that—no gravestones, not glamorous—away from the rest of the cemetery. I have an 'in' with them, so I'm sure it will be ok. They don't want to just cremate the guy?"

"Well, certain people in the building... felt bad when he died and... thought it would be best this way."

"Ah—of course."

"By any chance, are you free Friday?"

There was a pause.

"Well, it's got to be early—I mean no later than like 10:00 in the morning—I don't want to extend too far into the afternoon because of my Shabbat."

"Of course, 10 should work fine. I will confirm and get back to you."

"Oh Kev—don't forget—I'll need the signed death cert with raised seal and police report."

"Yes—I will have those." Kev realized he would need the signature of a licensed medical doctor on the death certificate. He had access to death certificates from the M.E.'s Office and had stashed several sealed originals at home. He could type one up. He had a momentary concern about where he would dredge up a legitimate medical doctor to sign the death certificate. And then he quickly remembered. He had a medical doctor currently residing in his garage. All good.

"And Kev—we are going to need a casket, too. We got an 'ok' one for the other guy 'cause of the donations, but do you remember the cheap ones I told you about? Do you want the cheapest of the cheapies?"

"Yes, the cheapest—I will have the money for it." Kev was

remembering it was around $300 which still seemed like a lot. Bhavna was going to wonder about where the $300 went to, but he'd find a way to explain it.

"Ok Kev."

Dixit gave Golding the address and clicked-off. He looked around again. He felt bad and really hated using his friends—especially a good guy like the Troll. But he knew it had to be done. This was a disaster. It was 'all hands on deck.'

He glanced through his phone menu and punched the number for Waxley.

The phone rang for a long time. He was about to hang up when he heard a loud voice. It sounded like someone yelping and then he realized it was Waxley singing: "Happy Thanksgiving my friend my friend—Happy Thanksgiving to you!!"

"Chris—is that you? It's Kev. Kev Dixit." The sound stopped.

"Oh, hey Kev—sorry for the crazy greeting, that was me doing the melody to 'I am a Pirate King!' How was it? Not bad? Well, I'm actually not doing the Pirate King part, but I am in the chorus!"

"Oh, hey Chris—that was something! Really glad to hear you still have it my man!"

"Woo, thanks, Kev. I am psyched! So, listen: tomorrow—Thanksgiving of course—I organized a bunch of us from the "Pirates" cast to go down to Bea Gaddy's and perform a few songs acapella! And—get this—the spot is going to be televised on channel 45! Can you believe it? They're doing a live feed during the afternoon after the high school football games and will do a cut-in of us doing the Major General's song! And guess who is sharing the lead? Yours truly! Woo hoo!"

"That's fantastic Chris!"

"And of course, our gang will be serving food to the homeless, so they'll be some good things going on, but what a great opportunity to get to perform—on the tube!"

"Yes, amazing!"

"We are calling our troupe the 'Sing For Our Supper Club.' Get it?"

"Yes—very cool!"

"We might do 'A Rollicking Band of Pirates We.' Not sure, yet—depends on the timing."

"Of course."

"Kev, now listen to this—I know it's a little crazy, but I am trying to get the real 'Captain Chesapeake' to perform with us tomorrow. Picture it: the 'Pirates of Penzance' led by Baltimore's own Captain Chesapeake! Outstanding! I don't know him personally, but one of the guys in the cast used to room with the guy that was Mondy the Sea Monster—you know, he was the guy that would be in the outfit. There were a few of them over the years."

"Yes."

"So, can you picture it? Captain Chesapeake—my hero—back on Chanel 45! Doing a song with me and our guys!"

"Sounds incredible!"

"Yes—I'm very stoked!"

"That's wonderful, Chris—really happy to hear it! Bhavna and I will be watching tomorrow!"

"Awesome, Kev!"

"So, Chris—I don't want to get too far ahead of things, but were you doing anything around 10 AM, Friday?"

• • •

Ricciti and Palanzo had returned with the supplies, five large, white plastic bags' worth.

"Kev, we were thinking. There's a security camera in the

elevator that records everything and it's time coded, so we thought we'd better be careful about how we get... the body... out of here."

"Oh, ok Lou—good thinking. We'll use the stairs for that."

They handed the plastic bags over to Kev, who checked to see what they had gotten. He put the bags down on a safe spot on the floor.

Palanzo said: "Don't be pissed about the sweatshirts."

Dixit reached in and retrieved a shirt. It said 'Monster Truck Rally' in oversized comic book lettering. The shirt featured an enormous full color cartoon of two 'monster trucks' simultaneously jumping a bunch of barrels in different directions. The trucks were dayglow orange and psychedelic eggplant purple. The orange one had spidery lettering on the side that said 'Wheelie King.' The purple one featured sinister lettering that said 'Da Bomb.' The barrels were neon green with black 'toxic' skull and crossbones symbols. Smoke was billowing from the tailpipes of the trucks.

Dixit left the tag on, removed his patrolman's cap and pulled his shirt over his head. It covered the top part of his police uniform. He put his cap back on and looked down at himself and chuckled. "Haute couture...."

"What, Kev?"

"No—these are fine."

Ricciti scowled. "I got the cheapest ones—these were on sale. I told you Pete, Kev wouldn't care!"

Dixit handed out the other identical sweatshirts to the two. He waited for them to get their shirts on. Then he opened the box of green plastic trash bags. "Did you guys get only one box?"

Ricciti barked: "Yeah, Kev, because they only had this one box of green plastic trash bags. The other ones were those smaller, white ones. And they had a lot of boxes of those green 'lawn and leaf' bags. But, you said 'green plastic trash bags' so we just got the one."

Dixit wondered how the two managed to graduate from Ignatius High. "Ok, do like this." He unfolded a bag and carefully poked a hole with his thumb into the center of the bottom. Then he forced the hole open a little bigger with his hands and fingers. He removed his cap and squeezed the bag over his head and over his torso, like a poncho.

"Now I need a couple arm holes." He estimated the best spots for arm holes and carefully ripped open the bag along the sides, manipulating his arms through the slits, giving the appearance of a low rent Houdini performing the straight jacket stunt.

The other two followed suit.

Dixit then distributed the gallon storage bags. He sat down at a safe spot on the floor next to the bags. He opened one of the duct tape packs and tore off several inches. He slipped a bag over his right shoe and taped the bag shut to his pants leg of his uniform. He followed with the other foot. "See?"

He tossed the tape over to Ricciti. Ricciti started with his left shoe. He pulled out a foot or so of tape. He tried to use the plastic cutting mechanism built into the dispenser, but quickly gave up and ripped the end with his teeth.

Dixit looked over, bemused. "Ok Lou—do you have scissors somewhere, because you're not going to want to do that all day."

"Sure, Kev. But they're in that top drawer." The corpse was blocking access to the drawer.

"Ok. We'll get to the drawer in a minute." The two followed suit, creating their own sandwich bag galoshes.

Next Dixit gave out the yellow, vinyl dishwashing gloves.

Palanzo was quickly struggling. "Geez, my fuckin' hands are

too big for these."

"It's the biggest size they had, dickhead. Just keep trying."

"Ok, Lou."

Palanzo finally squeezed the gloves on.

Dixit had already made his way over to the corpse. He took a closer look at the mangled handgun lying on the blood-soaked carpet below the desk. He left it there for the moment. He gently manipulated corpse's head to see the neck wound. It was large. Blood was still trickling from the gash. He looked over at the two. "Pete. Get another trash bag open. We'll use it for trash. Lou, tear off about 4 or 5 paper towels."

Dixit took the towels and carefully blotted up as much blood as possible from the wound area. Palanzo instinctively held open the trash bag for Dixit. "Thanks Pete. Now, Lou, get the duct tape and tear-off about a yard—and hand it over here, please."

Ricciti pulled out a few feet of tape and again ripped the end with his teeth. "Here you go, Kev."

Dixit began wrapping the duct tape around the corpse's neck. "Give me another yard, Lou."

Ricciti tore off another chunk and handed it over to Dixit, who carefully laid down another layer around its neck.

"I think that's going to hold."

The sight of Dixit wrapping the duct tape tourniquet made Palanzo queasy. He looked away.

Dixit moved the office chair and corpse back a bit and opened the desk drawer. He motioned to Ricciti. "Lou, your hands are still clean. Reach over and grab the scissors."

He carefully reached over Dixit into the desk drawer for the scissors. He was thinking back to when he had stashed Pete's gun in the drawer and was damned glad that Dixit thought it belonged to Willoughby.

"Ok Lou. Pull out like four of the trash bags. Cut the side and bottom of each bag open to turn the bag into like one big sheet—like four beach towels."

Ricciti cut the bags as directed. Palanzo was also on his knees, helping to place the bags, side by side. After Ricciti had done so, Dixit said: "Ok Lou, tape them together, side by side, to make one big towel."

Ricciti pointed down to the bags. "Hold them together Pete so I can tape. Here and here."

Palanzo awkwardly held the pieces down.

"Not like that, dickhead—I don't want to tape your hands to the bag! Use your fucking fingers!"

Eventually, they finished.

At Dixit's direction, Dixit and Ricciti tried hoisting the corpse out of the chair. The operation was tricky because the office chair kept moving with the body, making removal difficult.

Ricciti was grunting against the weight. "Fuckin' heavy bastard! Fuckin' chair keeps moving!"

Dixit planted a foot onto the wheeled part of the chair to keep it still. "Pete, come over and help Lou."

Palanzo gingerly made his way over to the chair and helped Ricciti pull at the corpse's torso. The two clumsily maneuvered the body out of the office chair and laid it onto the trash bag mosaic. Pete quicky got up and retreated back several paces.

"Ok, this is the body bag. We're going to roll the body up into this." Pete stayed back and watched as Dixit and Ricciti lifted the prone body over to the end part of the bag towel.

"Lou, cut like four strips of tape—about a foot, each." Dixit held out his hands, approximating the tape length.

This time, Ricciti used the scissors. He handed two of the cut strips over to Palanzo. "Here Pete. Hold these two. I can't hold 'em all!"

Dixit laid the end of the plastic sheet along the corpse and received the tape strips, taping the bag to the corpse's torso at four points along its body. "Now, Lou, help me roll him over."

Ricciti and Dixit began rolling the body into the plastic sheet. After a few turns, Ricciti would cut off more strips and they would tape the sheet along the head and feet to keep it more snug.

Finally, they completed the task.

"Jesus Kev, he looks like a fuckin' tootsie roll."

Palanzo said: "I was about to say saltwater taffy!"

Dixit looked down at the effort. "Not quite good enough. I can see that this is a dead guy—here's the head, pretty obviously, and here's the feet."

He had nodded his head in the direction of the head and feet as he spoke. "We need to make this an undiscernible mass. You know—people seeing this shouldn't know it's a dead guy."

Ricciti spoke: "Yeah right Kev. Should we get more bags?"

They had used all the bags in the box.

"Yeah—you guys get your protective gear off and head back to the CVS. Get a large sized box of 'lawn and leaf' bags and two more duct tapes."

The two began to remove their trash bag ponchos.

"Kev, could I keep the sweatshirt on? It's one less thing to do."

"Well, Pete, it's still got the price tag on it, so they might have you arrested for shoplifting. Then they'd call me and I'd have to take my sweatshirt off and go down there to bail you out."

Dixit was smiling. Palanzo looked on blankly.

Ricciti said, "that means take the fuckin' shirt off, Pete!"

"Oh—ok! Geez...."

•••

It was nearly 4 o'clock and almost dark outside. Dixit was alone again in the office. He looked down at the shrouded mass on the floor. He looked around at the rest of horrific scene. He felt miserable.

He was thinking, 'here I am, again trying to spin an impossible situation into something manageable—something palatable.' He was thinking that maybe that's all his life had ever been—all he had amounted to? A series of deflections and feints and white lies and downright lies as he tried to navigate—tried to survive— his everyday life. Always trying to turn something obviously black and white into something grey, because that's where his life resided now. Always in the land of 'grey,' where there were never any absolutes. No real 'rights' no real 'wrongs.' How had he gotten to be like that? To be that person? To live in that world?

He didn't want to be that person—always massaging the truth, always trying to avoid unavoidable consequences.

He glanced again at the body.

Ricciti and Palanzo had gotten themselves in deep with a monster. He would do what he could to protect them. He would have a long talk with them about their business associations, later.

And he was thinking that he had to have done the right thing for Melody. He would never let a fellow cop be wrung through the same wringer that churned him to bits after his first killing. He remembered back to the first Department shrink—what was the guy's name? Dr. Nillson? What absolute crap. Having to relive the shooting, over and over, looking for 'insights' about his feelings—his motives. 'Motives' like preventing an enraged animal from killing a powerless victim... What was so hard to understand? The guy just couldn't understand that he did not want to kill the guy—but he had to.

And the endless 'psychological' tests—they all tried to trip you up by leading you to a response. He hated it all. No, sparing Jurgen from that was the right thing to do. She would eventually be cut loose as his rookie partner and probably face her own 'line of duty' killing in the future—but he will have least spared her this time.

And then he thought: 'thank God for Bhavna.' In the end, the sessions with the shrink worked out for him. Nillson couldn't make that one session—there was a new stand-in: Dr. Bhavna Sarija. When she first entered the room, his breath was taken away. She was so beautiful. And she was so kind and understanding—the exact opposite of Nillson. He was able to have Bhavna assigned to his case thanks to his guy in Human Resources. He fell in love with her after just a few sessions. He could sense that she felt something for him, too. Psychotherapy sessions with Bhavna were like dates—plenty of laughter and down to earth conversations. They talked about so many things—their cultural backgrounds as persons of Indian descent, what it was like growing up in Baltimore, how his family wound up Catholic, the foods they loved, the places they'd been...

She told him that he was absolutely fit for duty—and had been from day one—but that she couldn't help but extend the sessions for a few weeks because she enjoyed his company so much.

He was in heaven. They became engaged almost immediately.

He looked around at the scene again. Thinking about meeting Bhavna had cheered him up, greatly.

And then he heard something. A sound—like a purring sound almost, but louder—now like a moaning sound...

He looked towards the source of the sound and saw movement in the bag. He couldn't believe what he was seeing. Willoughby was moving, writhing, within the bag. The moaning sound was getting louder and louder and the movements of the bag were increasing. Willoughby was trying to get free of the bag—trying to roll over... He saw Willoughby's arms pushing against the sides of the bag... he heard the muffled moans getting louder...

Dixit looked around and instinctively grabbed the first hard object within reach—a coffee mug from Ricciti's desk. The cup said, 'I Love Daddy.' He grasped the mug in his now trembling hand and brought it down with thunderous force onto the 'head' of the bag.

The cup 'clonked' upon the impact of the vicious strike, broke free from the handle and rolled across the floor to the corner of the room. Dixit was left holding the ceramic, broken-off handle.

He put the handle back on the desktop and went over to inspect the bag. It was definitely dead, now. He pushed and prodded it with his foot. He kicked at it some more. There was no life. He retrieved the broken cup from the floor and placed it next to the handle.

He took a deep breath and stood, looking over green bag. He nudged it with his foot a few more times. There was nothing.

Then it occurred to him—'Jurgen didn't kill the guy, after all. I did!' He chuckled to himself — all that time he was trying to justify preventing Jurgen from going through the horrors of her 'first kill.' And he wound up being the killer! He sighed to himself.

He felt bad—this was now his third killing. Where would it end? He began to search his conscience. He wanted to feel remorse for the man's death by his hand. But he didn't. He just couldn't dredge up any sympathy for guy. Try as he might, he couldn't help but thinking: 'the world is not going to miss another child molesting psychopath.' And then he thought: 'oh well, three time's the charm.' He chuckled to himself.

He was feeling better, now—more of his old self. He'd have to explain to Lou that he had been admiring Lou's mug and dropped it. And that he would get it fixed for him, asap, with some super glue...

• • •

January, 1997

The holidays passed and collapsed into the doldrums of January. Dixit had been working as much overtime as he could get in December. But January meant less traffic, fewer parades, less road rage, fewer family altercations, less shoplifting, fewer concerts and pageants—less everything. So, he was back to normal hours on Patrol. He had been working his way, mentally, through past events. Finding Willoughby's police record stashed away under the piles on that cop's desk left him feeling unsatisfied. The file had not been signed out and it was almost by luck that he had even found it. The cop was a detective in the CID. Why had he stashed Willoughby's jacket? He remembered the barroom napkin with addresses scrawled in ballpoint. He hadn't thought much about it then. He had just enough time that day to learn that Willoughby was a vicious sociopath with a long record. But now he was curious about the cop, the file and the addresses.

Ricciti and Palanzo had claimed to know nothing of Willoughby's past. They told him that their company did real estate and that Willoughby had come along as part of a corporate reshuffle. But then, after the merger, Willoughby had tried to take over everything through threats and intimidation. He kind of believed them, more or less. But he could tell that there was more to the story.

He decided to visit the CID bullpen that Saturday morning

when most of the detectives would be out or off-duty. He had checked earlier in the week to see if Willoughby's file had been returned. It wasn't. He wandered through the bullpen and over towards the desk of the cop who had stashed the jacket. Dixit was in street clothes and the few clerical workers around the bullpen took no particular notice of his presence. The cop was out. The cop still had several large piles on his slovenly desktop. Dixit carefully rifled through the paper mountain. But they were by all appearances current case files. Willoughby's jacket was nowhere to be found.

He quietly pulled-open the desk drawers, but found no files, just piles of pens, markers, ratty porn magazines and leftover trash. He wandered past the few other desks in the bullpen with stacks of files and began checking them out. One of the employees looked up from his monitor and began staring Dixit's way. But he just gave the guy a friendly wave and went about his search. It was a wasted effort. The file was not to be found.

He was thinking back to the scrawled addresses on the napkin. He did recall a few of them because they were all on the unit block of the same street—Algarth. He remembered at the time that the numbers were the same as his bike's combination lock. And he remembered another one because he used to stop at the sub shop on that street—Glendon—and the address was the same number as his home address. It was probably a mile east of the sub shop, though. And he thought of one more. He had responded to an assault on that street and remembered because it was his first case where lye was thrown onto the face of the victim— McCready Avenue. And he remembered that the number was in that same area—probably next door or a couple doors down? He could probably find it.

He didn't want to take time away from his home life, but he

decided that he would check out the addresses in the evenings, when he would go off-duty, just before heading home.

• • •

Dixit drove past this one, the last address. All the other homes had been destroyed by fires. This one was not a burnout like the others, but it looked abandoned. As he drove by, he glanced around at the collection of boarded-up, graffitied rowhouses. There were only a few homes on the block that looked habitable.

He pulled a u turn at the end of the street and parked across from the house. At 6:30 PM in January, it was dark. And cold. He grabbed a flashlight from his glove box and walked across the street to the house. The 'door' was plywood with a rope pull for a door knob. There was no lock. He could tell the marble steps hadn't been scrubbed in decades. The first-floor windows were cracked but not completely broken because they had been reinforced with iron rails. The vandals could only inflict so much damage to the windows.

He moved cautiously to the door. He felt a little foolish rapping on the plywood. He gingerly pulled the rope and opened the door. He shined his flashlight in and called out "hello?" The place smelled foul. He moved the light around. He saw the trashed paraphernalia and could tell the place had been a shooting gallery. He carefully entered and gave a few more "hellos." He heard some rats scurrying away from his flashlight. The farther he entered the worse the smell became—an unbearable stench of stale urine and human feces.

He had seen enough. As he turned around to retreat, he saw a tall man just inside the doorway entrance—blocking his exit. The man was holding his nose with one hand and pointing a gun at

Dixit with the other one.

"What you doin' here, mon?"

The voice had a Jamaican accent. He saw the man's long dreads in the shadow, outlined against the dull street light outside. Before Dixit could muster an answer, the guy took his hand away from his nose. He now had both hands on the gun trained on Dixit.

"Put that flashlight down!" He pointed the gun down towards the ground.

Dixit carefully placed the light down onto the filthy floor.

"Now, I said, dirty cop, what you doin' here?"

Dixit was unarmed. He began to tremble. He was wondering how the guy knew he was a cop. He was in street clothes.

"Hey man—it's cool—I'm just checking the place out. I was just leaving, man. Sorry to intrude." He was holding his arms up to signify surrender. He began walking slowly towards the entrance.

The man kept the gun trained directly on Dixit.

"Stay where you are dirty cop. I asked you why you here, dirty cop? I know you are a cop and I know you are a dirty cop—because otherwise you would not be here."

Dixit gulped. He was puzzled about the 'dirty' part. He put his arms down to his sides.

"Hey look man, I am a cop, ok. But why are you calling me a 'dirty' cop?"

The man with the gun laughed quietly. "Because I am a cop. And I know you are a dirty cop because I have been following you, dirty cop. That is how."

Dixit was having a hard time believing what he was hearing.

"You're a cop? If you're a cop, show me your badge?"

The man pulled the gun up more stiffly, as though about to

squeeze a round off. "I'll show you nothing, motherfucker! I am a cop—but not much longer. I am sick of dealing with you shitty people!"

Dixit could tell the guy was getting angrier.

He tried to calm him down by waving his hands before him as though to massage away the palpable level of stress in the filthy house.

"Hey man. It's cool. It's cool. I'm a cop. But I'm not a 'dirty' cop. I'm here to check out addresses I found in the file of a psycho—that was stashed away on a cop's desk. I don't even know the cop. I'm a Patrol officer. That's why I needed the guy's jacket. There was a... disturbance involving the guy."

The man now held the gun in his right hand and brought it down to his side. But he was still standing and blocking the way to the exit.

"Ok. But why d'you care about these houses? Why you been checking them out?"

Dixit let his own hands drop. "Because I was suspicious about why that cop had the guy's jacket and was basically hiding it. It wasn't signed out and..."

He didn't want to tell the guy that the psycho met his end at Dixit's own hand.

"You were suspicious of the cop, Hayman?"

"Well, I didn't even know his name. But, if that's the guy, yes, why did he hide the guy's jacket? The file is still missing. I came to these houses because they're the only ones I remembered on that paper napkin. I was just trying to figure out what was going on."

• • •

Friday, September 11, 2015
She noticed the handsome cop looking her over—quite a bit.

She was having a little trouble remembering all the names, being her first day in CID. Being plainclothes, no one was wearing IDs. Now the lanky cop with perfect hair—really perfect, tight rows—was coming her way. What a face, too...

"Aquanetta—is that you? What ya doin' here?"

Dinetta stood and shook the man's hand. "No, no, I'm Dinetta. My sister is Aquanetta. You must have met her working in the Bail Commissioner's Office?"

"Yes—yes! Oh Lord, the resemblance is like crazy! Are you two twins?" He was smiling so nicely... he had nice teeth, too...

"No, no—we get that all the time. We almost could be. But she's my little sister—about 14 months younger than me."

"Oh, wow—ok! Amazing!"

There was an awkward pause as they stood together.

"Oh—I am Bonaventure. Been in CID about three years now."

There was another pause.

He said: "So, do you know—is Aquanetta seeing anybody? Does she have a man?" Bonaventure felt a little embarrassed, having asked. But he wanted to know.

"Well, she's not married or engaged, but she has a boyfriend right now—but, who knows—right?"

She thought, 'damn Aquanetta, get rid of the lazy ass of a boyfriend because I have got a real guy for you!' She knew their Baptist mom would be ecstatic if Aquanetta would ditch that turd. He had moved in with Aquanetta, and Mother did not approve of the situation—at all.

There was another awkward pause. Dinetta took a breath, "so, how do you like being in CID? How has it been?"

"Well, it is all crazy—all the time! But we all work really hard. It's a grind, but I like it! Good parts are investigating—boring stuff is trials—but, it all has to be done, right?"

"Yes... Detective Dixit was telling me about it all. He seems like a good guy to be paired with."

Bonaventure sighed. "Yes—Kev is ok, he's ok. But—be a little careful, ok?"

She looked on, puzzled. Bonaventure moved closer and said, quietly, "not everyone up here is like Kev. Just be a little careful up here. Be watchful. Kev is ok. But the others—you know? Ok?"

She felt a little shocked by what he was implying—but then he quickly flashed that smile and said: "But you tell Aquanetta... Aurelio, you know—Bonaventure—says 'hello!'"

• • •

August, 1998

He had been working the usual day on the streets. And then he heard his badge called-out from Dispatch.

"Detective 10869, 10869: 10-62. Repeat 10-62."

'Shit, now what...' he thought.

He pulled into a filling station on Eastern Avenue. He clicked his radio and called into Dispatch.

"Dixit—10869—what's up?"

"Detective Dixit. We've received a message. Stand by."

He felt his heart racing. He was thinking about his boy and those damned food allergies. Otherwise, Vadin was perfectly normal and in good shape—well adjusted. Had something happened to his boy? Or his Bhavna? Why was he receiving an urgent dispatch?

"You've got a priority message from one Louis Ricciti, repeat Louis Ricciti—in Central Booking. He asks you to 'come and find him.' He and a 'Pete Paletzo' are arrested—says to 'help him.'"

Dixit began to sweat. That was almost the last thing he

wanted to hear. "Ok. Got it. Thanks."

He sat back in his car seat and clicked-off the engine. Shit. What had those two blockheads done, now? He momentarily thought about the dead guy—was that it? Had they been arrested in connection with that guy—maybe about him being missing? And then he thought, 'no' couldn't be. No one out there would have ever given a shit about that guy. It had to be something else.

He drove to Central Booking and thought back to that lousy day. If it was about the dead guy, he was thinking that there were post-mortem contractions and sounds associated with a dead body. Perhaps the guy wasn't alive? If not under oath, he could suggest the possibility of such? A person couldn't be held accountable for killing a guy who was already dead?

His hands were now sweating on the wheel. The problem was, he knew in his heart that the guy was still alive. He might have actually been able to save the guy's life... Why didn't he? He sighed to himself. He was thinking that if he were under oath, he would have to tell the truth. He could massage the truth other-wise—but he was not going to be able to lie under oath. That was the bottom line.

He would simply have to tell them: 'it just seemed like the right thing to do at the time.'

And then he calmed himself. It was not going to be about the dead guy.

• • •

He had been to Central Booking and Intake a thousand times. He learned from 'Visitor Information' that Ricciti was just then meeting with his lawyer. They told him that Ricciti had ok'd Dixit sitting-in on his attorney conference. He found his way over to the row of meeting cubicles. He flashed his badge and was allowed entrance.

He had seen that guy's face before—the attorney. But where? The man rose and introduced himself.

"You're Officer... Kev Dixit? Hey—I'm Joey Reed, representing our boy, Lou!"

Joey attempted a hip 'high five' but settled for a handshake when Dixit seemed confused.

Dixit knew he'd seen this guy before, somewhere. The carrot-colored suntan, the pitch-black, dyed hair and the mouthful of frighteningly white veneers.

"Nice to meet you, Mr. Reed." Dixit took a seat next to Reed and looked across the table to Ricciti, who was handcuffed to the hook in the floor.

"So, Lou, what are the charges?"

Ricciti scowled.

"Un-fucking believable, Kev." He inhaled deeply. "Theft, embezzlement, mortgage fraud, kickbacks, conspiracy, and a bunch of other lies like that!"

Joey Reed shook his head in agreement. "Officer—it's all bullshit. 'White collar' stuff. Complete bullshit. Nothing we can't handle. In fact, I intend to make an example of the State's Attorney for even indicting with this trash!"

Dixit was thinking 'I wonder if this guy has actually handled a real trial in the last five... or ten years?' He had never seen the guy in the courthouse.

"Ok. Have you made bail, Lou?"

Joey answered, "We've got that Officer. I've got Muther Trucker's on it. Lou will be cut loose within the hour, as soon as Patsy gets over there."

"Yeah, Kev. Thank God for Patsy. She got me Joey because he's actually related by marriage. Joey is Patsy's step-brother's, uncle's second cousin."

Joey Reed smiled in agreement. The reflected blaze from his veneers caused Dixit to blink.

"Ok."

"Yeah, Kev, Joey handles exclusively criminal stuff, right Joey?"

Joey nodded, proudly. "Yes, exclusively criminal, with some estates and trusts and mineral rights law, too."

"Ok, what about Pete? You said he was arrested, too?"

Joey spoke: "Yes, but we've got that covered, Officer. My law partner, Rob Dona, is coming over to handle Pete's defense. We've got Funky Bruther's Bonds on that one."

Joey didn't think it appropriate to reveal that he and his law partner each owned their respective bail bond companies. 'Spread the joy' he was thinking.

Dixit was wondering about all of this.

"You know, you guys might have a conflict of interest—same firm representing both defendants?"

"Oh, absolutely, Officer, but we've built a 'Chinese Wall'—it's impenetrable. We will not have a conflict!"

Joey was nodding, proudly.

"Ok. But, Lou, you know, Skip Weller could be helpful? Remember Skip? He could maybe take Pete's case?"

Joey jumped in: "No need to worry Officer. We've got this. This is complete shit. We'll knock this out before it even gets to trial. Way before trial." Joey was nodding, firmly.

Dixit was watching Joey's head movements. And then he remembered where he saw the guy—the huge advertising placards on the sides of the MTA busses. All over town. On the placard, 'Joey' was seen grinning and waving the 'call me' thing with his hand to his ear. He was wearing a 'Miami Vice' teal sports coat and a black polyester tee shirt with a little gold chain around his neck. The chain had a little tiny coke spoon. His dyed hair and white teeth blazed forward. There appeared to be dandruff flakes on his lapels.

Dixit was remembering that the other guy on the bus placard, the law partner, Dona, looked about thirty years older—and definitely confused. It looked like the guy didn't even know his picture was being taken. There was a demented glaze in his eyes. His matted blonde toupee was a ludicrous fraud. He was wearing a weird looking large plaid sportscoat with a bulbous orange necktie. Deep green cacti were embedded into the necktie.

"So, Lou, this 'white collar' stuff? You guys were working in real estate, right? What do they think you were doing?"

Joey responded, quickly: "Officer, my client is not at liberty to speak to that right now. It will all come out in the wash. But, basically, Lou is being railroaded because he tried to assist an entire class of economically disadvantaged Baltimoreans buy their own homes. Yes. Can you believe that shit? The Clinton Administration made home ownership a priority in this country and guys like Lou and... and... what's his name, Lou? Your guy... you know, the other guy, your partner?"

"Pete."

"Pete... that's right... those guys make that possible for people and are now forced to suffer the consequences. All because of a political witch hunt orchestrated by Republican insiders within the State's Attorney's Office."

Dixit was thinking that Lou was definitely in trouble.

"So, Officer we're going to need you as a character witness for Lou."

Dixit sighed. "You bet."

• • •

April, 2014

He passed by Jackie seated in the hallway. She was reading her phone. She ignored him. Dixit was pretty sure she was Hayman's third wife. The scuttlebutt was that she had danced on the Block before hooking up with Hayman.

Dixit looked down at the shrunken frame of Hayman as he slept. He had eventually gotten used to Hayman. He had almost grown to like him. Almost. He had learned quite a bit from him during the time before Hayman retired. Seeing him wasting away in hospice care brought a lump to his throat. His eyes began to water. He had been visiting, almost daily and hadn't had a chance to speak with him. Hayman had always been sleeping.

He thought back to the plan he and St. Bonaventure had put together. They would retain the evidence they had on Hayman for use on a rainy day. Bonaventure would muster out of CID and go back to precinct work. If Bonaventure was threatened by Hayman or anyone in Hayman's circle, they would both turn Hayman in. They had developed enough evidence to put him away for years. They agreed that once Hayman was out of CID, should either get themselves in, they would lobby for the other.

Dixit was glad he never had to rat-out Hayman. Turning him in would have certainly opened up investigation of Hayman's associates, like Willoughby. 'Less said, the better.'

And, by fluke, he was pulled into the CID and partnered-up with Hayman, of all people, by the brass.

He saw that Hayman was waking. He leaned over the hospital bed. "Hey Chief. It's Kev."

He saw Hayman struggling, trying to move his hand. And then he saw—Hayman was giving him the finger.

Hayman then wiggled his middle finger to beckon Dixit closer. He was trying to say something. Dixit leaned his head in.

"What, boss?"

"Fuck you..."

And then he died.

Dixit stood back, a little shocked. Not quite the farewell he had expected. He left the room and looked down the hall to get Jackie, but she had apparently stepped away. He found a hospice nurse and then followed the nurse back into the room.

The nurse did a quick check for vitals. "Yes. I'm sorry, sir, he's passed. I'll go find the doctor so that he can pronounce."

"Ok—thank you."

Dixit continued to stand next to the bed, gazing down at Hayman. He heard the clacking sound of high heels approaching from the hallway. Jackie entered the room.

"They said Stan's dead?"

"Yes, I'm sorry Jackie, he just passed away."

"Were you speaking with him? Did he say anything?"

Dixit did a quick calculation: "Ah, yes—he said to tell you he loved you very much."

Jackie looked on blankly. "Bullshit, Dixit. Bullshit. He would never have said that. Stan always said that you were completely full of shit. Go fuck yourself."

• • •

September 5, 2017

The man sat quietly in his 2002 Ford Fiesta. He pulled a paper napkin from his shirt pocket and glanced at the address. He stuffed the paper back into his pocket. Looking at the address was a pointless act, born of anxiety. He had surveilled the neighborhood two days earlier in broad daylight. He didn't need the napkin. He glanced at his wristwatch: 2:00 AM. He clicked-off the dome light and latched his seatbelt into place.

The man wheeled the Fiesta away from the curb and began accelerating, forcing the gas pedal closer and closer to the floorboard. Midway down the street, the man calmly removed his eyeglasses, folded them, and placed them on the passenger's seat. The car pushed past 50 mph, rattling severely as it approached the end of the road. He edged the accelerator down to the floor. The steering wheel vibrated sharply in his hands under the strain, the meter wiggling at 62 mph. Inhaling deeply, he jerked the wheel wildly to the right, bouncing the car up over the curb and onto the sidewalk. His shoulder slammed painfully against the driver's side doorframe. Jamming the accelerator against the floor, he closed his eyes.

The front end of the car ripped into the fire hydrant, gouging the Fiesta's undersides. The collision broadcast the shrieking siren of metal on metal onto the quiet neighborhood. The seat harness tore into the man's frame, grabbing and bruising his spleen. Instantaneously, the white airbag mushroomed from the steering column, punching the man's face, bloodying his nose.

The car slammed violently into an earthen berm a few yards beyond the twisted metal remains of the hydrant. The man lost consciousness in the peaceful suburban geyser.

• • •

October, 2017

He heard his cell warble and looked to see the caller. Boyce. This would not be good.

"Hey Kev, it's Boyce. Ready for something special? I've got something really dope—just for you."

Dixit sighed to himself and looked down. His workload was killing him.

"Ah, ok Sarge. What special 'dope' thing do you have for

me—a raise?"

"Ha ha! Very good Kev. No. What I have is better. A little 'cloak and dagger'—just the kind of thing you like!"

Boyce knew Dixit was not going to like it—at all. Dixit was already handling an enormous caseload, thanks to Boyce. But the FBI guy specified Dixit by name. So, too bad, Dixit. 'Tag. You're it.'

"Well, it's best to explain it in person. It's a liaise with the FBI on a sensitive but interesting matter. Tomorrow, 10 AM, HQ. See you in my office—tomorrow. Bye."

Dixit was about to respond that he had a bunch of other things that would conflict, but he saw that Boyce had clicked-off.

• • •

Dixit arrived at Boyce's office. A man in a dark blue suit was already seated in front of Boyce's desk. Boyce rose from his seat to make introductions. The man in the dark blue suit also stood, formally.

"Agent Markai, this is Detective Kev Dixit."

"Detective Dixit? I am Mar, Kai. Very pleased to make your acquaintance."

Handshakes were exchanged. Kev couldn't help notice that the agent was wearing a clip-on necktie. The three sat down.

There was a substantial pause.

Boyce looked around to each and said: "So, what is the name of the subject... or person of interest, if that is the appropriate term?"

"His name is Herman... Miller."

There was another pause.

Dixit was thinking it was oddly coincidental. Bhavna had been extolling the virtue of those chairs. But they did not own one. The chairs were pricey.

"Do you mean, Herman Miller—the chair guy?"

Agent Markai looked on, puzzled. "Chairs? I don't believe so, sir. No. I meant, surname, Herman; given name Miller. He goes by 'Miller Herman.'"

Boyce and Dixit looked at each other, puzzled.

"So, the guy's name is Miller Herman?"

"Yes."

There was another substantial pause. Boyce looked over to Dixit and Dixit stared back at Boyce.

"So, Agent Markai, what is it we should know about Miller Herman?"

"I wouldn't know."

Boyce looked over to Dixit for moral support. He was starting to lose patience.

"Ok Agent Markai—what do you want to tell us about Herman—what should we be looking into?"

There was a pause.

"Well, I'm not at liberty to disclose that. I was only authorized to provide you the name... and then, only if asked."

Boyce's chest heaved in exasperation.

Dixit thought, 'who the hell is this guy—how the hell old is he? He looks like a kid.'

"But if you can't tell us anything, why did the Bureau arrange the meeting?"

"Well, I'm not sure why."

Boyce realized he was grinding his teeth again.

Dixit turned in his seat and looked directly at the agent. "Ok. Are you actually an agent? I think the Bureau only takes college grads—and usually with a graduate degree, too? You can't be that old. What's going on, here?"

"Oh, I have a BA from Georgetown and a MS in Criminal Justice from USC. But I'm 16 and too young to be an agent. I'm an Intern in the Mentorship Program."

Boyce looked over to Dixit. "Kev, they said you knew this agent? 'Markey or Marklay.'"

Dixit looked down, in thought. "Let me guess—your last name is 'Mar' and your first name is 'Kai?' Your name is Kai Mar, not Markai?"

"Yes sir, that is correct."

"Was an Agent Reginald Marquis supposed to meet us?" Kev was thinking that Reg was the only guy he really knew within the FBI.

"Yes, of course."

"Ok. Where is Agent Marquis?"

"He is here."

Boyce was now looking up at the ceiling and shaking his head in disbelief. He looked back down.

"He's here? What—did he stop into the restroom on the way up?"

Kai Mar looked flabbergasted.

"Certainly not. He's not in the building."

"Ok—where is Agent Marquis, exactly?"

"Didn't they tell you? He always stays in the staff car. That way he can continue to work rather than waste time on unnecessary movement. You're required to meet with him in the staff car. I'm his driver. I have a District of Columbia driver's license."

Boyce was looking up at the ceiling again. He looked back down.

"Why didn't you set us straight and tell us you're not an agent?"

"My Program Advisor told me that I needed to stop

correcting others. It's one of my perceived character flaws. So, I am limited to three corrections per day, which I self-report. I didn't want to waste a correction on a minor thing."

• • •

The three walked over to the garage parking lot. Kai Mar pressed the 5th floor elevator button. Dixit and Boyce saw the black sedan idling one aisle over. They approached the sedan, but noticed that Kai Mar had stopped a few paces behind. They looked back, quizzically.

"Why are you going there? Agent Marquis is here." He pointed to a candy apple red Prius.

Kai Mar opened the rear passenger doors of the Prius for the guests, but stayed outside, eventually leaning against the rear of the car.

Boyce and Dixit squeezed into the back and saw Marquis in the front passenger's side seat busily working from his tablet. Five other tablets were strategically Velcroed to the dash and windshield area in front of his passenger's seat.

Marquis finally became aware of movement and craned his head towards the back seat. "Hey Kev! You're here? And you must be Sergeant Malcolm Boyce? Thanks so much for meeting with me!"

Half-hearted handshakes over and around the safety headrests were attempted. Marquis had not relinquished possession of his tablet.

"So, you met my driver, Kai? Great kid!

"Yes, Reg—apparently a pretty smart kid, too!"

"I recruited him. I could not beat him playing online Quadra-Hex... you know, quadra-hexa-dimensional chess - and I knew he had the right mind for the Bureau!"

"That's great Reg."

Boyce's very bald head kept rubbing up against the ceiling of the car. He was too tall and it was too damned cramped. He was thinking if the agent in the passenger's seat had decided to sit in the back with them, they'd have a certifiable clown car. He was glad the agent didn't.

"So, Reg—what can we help you with?"

Reg, brought down the sun visor. He adjusted the vanity mirror so that he could see his passengers in the back seat.

"Ok. Here's what we have. We are investigating one Miller Herman. We believe he is running a Ponzi type, pyramid scheme selling variable annuities through several of his companies."

"Ok."

"The products are specious and their value utterly dependent on future buyers buying-in and funding present pay-outs."

"Understood."

"We believe that he is misappropriating and diverting funds into literally thousands of shell entities. I won't bore you with those details, but each shell has multiple shells, which in turn have multiple shells—and so on. We have our best forensic people on it but the work is laborious. It will take months—maybe a year or more to develop a case against him."

"Ok."

"So, he also invests a lot of 'his' money in the stock market. He recently had a huge margin call and had to scramble to pull together about $5 million cash to meet his shorts. Coincidently, around the same time, one of his properties, his Baltimore County mansion, suffered a complete loss from a fire. He had insurance and the property was 'free and clear,' so he stood to grab policy limits of about $6 million. We believe that the funds used to purchase the home a few years ago were tainted and that the home purchase was just another way for him to launder money misappropriated through his scheme. Basically, he'd be washing-out his shorts with the insurance money."

Boyce was hoping that Dixit was 'getting' all this. He certainly wasn't. His wife washed his shorts every Thursday. That's about all he knew.

"But his plan was blocked by the insurance company. The company refused to pay out. Herman and the company are now in a civil suit about the policy."

"The company alleged arson?"

"Well, not specifically—the company alleged that the damage was not caused by an accident covered by its policy. But, reading between the lines, yes, that's the heart of the matter. The County Police investigated and determined the fire to be accidental. The company felt otherwise. We have the company's complaint filed with the court, but it only mentions 'circumstances inconsistent with an accidental fire.' Nothing more specific. We're not entirely sure what those 'circumstances' are."

"But if there's a lawsuit going on, wouldn't the insurance company have to give specifics?"

"Yes, eventually. But the insurance company filed the case to place the $6 million with the court—to be held until the court ruled on whether the fire was accidental or not. So, there will be a whole discovery process and back and forth before those theories start coming out."

"Ok. But why does the FBI care about this guy's arson?"

"Well, we'd love to see an arrest made by somebody—for something, anything. An arrest may shake the confidence of some of his investors and potential investors. The more pressure on Herman, the better. If he starts getting careless it will help us."

"But why do you need us?"

"Well, the Bureau doesn't have jurisdiction over garden variety arson. If our involvement is requested, sure, we have an entire unit of arson investigators to help locals. But otherwise, we can't be involved. I need a very discrete investigator to make an independent evaluation. If that investigator concludes that the fire was arson, we have a contact within the local government—also very discrete—willing to place appropriate pressure on the Police to reopen the investigation."

"Ok."

"So, Kev, obviously, I'm hoping you'll help me? It would be completely unofficial."

Dixit looked over to Boyce.

"Sure, Kev. What you do on your own time is your own business."

Dixit was thinking, 'my own time? Great.'

"Ok Reg. Did you want me to start with the insurance company people? Get their take on it?"

"No—no way. Sorry Kev. You can't contact the insurer. We can't tip our hand. We don't want anyone to know of our interest in Herman. And that means you can't contact the County Police or Fire Department about the fire. They're all off limits. None of those parties can know anything about an outside investigation. I can't even show this to our own arson guys."

"Ah, ok—what exactly did you want me to do, then?"

"Here—everything we have is on this." He reached around and handed Dixit a thumb drive. "It's the County Fire Department's Incident Report, the Fire Marshall's Investigator's report, the Police Report, the insurance company's court pleadings in the civil case, photos, house plans, etc. Everything you'll need."

Dixit looked at the drive and dropped it into his sports coat pocket. "What about sniffing around generally talking to neighbors, going out and checking the scene?"

"Well, you're going to have to be extremely careful. If in your judgment speaking with any given person would not in any way get back to Herman or his lawyers or lead back to us, ok. But otherwise, stay clear."

"How about help from our own people?" He gestured towards Boyce.

"No—this is all on you, Kev. I'm really sorry Sergeant Boyce."

Boyce felt greatly relieved.

Dixit thought, 'and why am I doing this?'

Boyce joined in, "Kev, you should know a few things about arson? You teamed with Hayman for a while back then? He handled a lot of arson, right?"

Dixit thought, 'Well, that's an understatement.'

"Well, a little..."

There was an uncomfortable silence.

"You know Reg, even if this pans out and the County makes the arrest, Herman will make bail and then probably skip—right?"

"Yes—and that would actually be helpful. Bail jumping is a crime in Maryland."

"They'd have to find him?"

"Sure, but we can help local police find fugitives travelling across state lines. We're actually pretty good at that."

There was another awkward silence.

"So, Reg, if the fire was determined to be accidental—what was the 'accident?'"

"Oh, right—the Fire Department reported that the home was struck by lightning." At that, Boyce involuntarily looked up to the ceiling in disbelief, bonking his forehead, creating a dull 'thump.'

"Lightning? And how is that possibly arson?"

"Well, that's the thing. We don't know. The insurance company thinks it was arson. That's a good start. But you'll see the Investigator's conclusion that lightning most likely struck the home and ignited embers within the building frame while rupturing a gas line inside. The report says that gas likely began pooling inside the home and was ultimately ignited by the burning embers. Apparently, there was quite an explosion in that part of the home. It is—or was—a pretty massive structure."

"So, no one was injured? Let me guess—Herman was not in the home at the time?"

"Correct. His alibi is airtight. He had tickets to a show in DC and was seen in attendance by several witnesses. He used his credit card to pay for the show and for dinner earlier that evening—again, confirmed by the waiter, manager and several diners. Apparently, one of his neighbors texted him about the fire while he was in the theater and by the time he got back, the home was a total loss. All of that is on the drive."

Dixit looked down at his folded hands. "When do you need this?"

"Yesterday, of course." Marquis was not smiling.

There was another silence.

Marquis then made a broad beckoning motion with his arm. Kai Mar came around and opened the rear doors of the Prius. The meeting was apparently over.

"Thanks again, Sergeant Boyce." Marquis reached back past the headrest and offered a tangled handshake to Boyce, who was carefully extracting his frame from the backseat.

"Kai, please accompany Sergeant Boyce back inside. Kev, could you please hang back and I'll give you my contact information."

"You know, Agent Marquis, I can find my own way back?"

Boyce was ignored. He gave up and let Kai Mar walk him back to the garage elevator.

"So, Kev—I wanted to thank you for this and also for all your and Bhavna's help and support for my... sabbatical."

"Oh, hey man, you've already thanked us a few hundred times! You're welcome! We're just glad you're in a better situation. It looks like this is working out for you!"

Dixit wished that Reg had found an entirely different career path, away from the FBI - but at least he seemed a little better.

"Yes—much, much better!"

Marquis handed Dixit a carefully folded index card. A number was typed on the card. It looked like it was typed on a 70's era IBM Selectric.

"Only phone this number. And please use a land line."

• • •

Brad checked his hair and skin tone, again, in the foyer mirror. Hair was still 'good.' He pinched his cheeks. He walked over, again, to the window. He had looked out the window a dozen times hoping for someone to show up at the open house—someone, anyone with a pulse, any warm body—please—any human besides another nosy neighbor. The last one was an incredibly talkative old bitch. And she brought her fucking annoying, yappy French poodle. The woman's face resembled the dog's—very pinched and weird. Exact same hairstyle. He forgot the woman's name but remembered the dog's name. "Mee Maw." 'What kind of name was "Mee Maw" for a dog?'

He thought he saw something out of the corner of his eye and glanced out the window. A woman in an orange and aquamarine sari and an older-looking man in a blue sports coat and grey slacks coming up the walk. He did a quick calculation: 'Low-key, highly skilled micro-surgeon and doting spouse. Foreign... Indian... and with money... Yes!'

He waited for them to enter, but they did not. He listened and thought he heard a gentle rapping at the front door. 'The guy thought he had to knock at an open house? The sign says 'open house.' Great. Hopeless.'

He opened the door and saw the Indian looking man and the woman, dutifully standing behind him.

"Hello—this house is... for sale?"

"Yes sir, it is, it is. I'm Brad. Please come in!"

"Kev Dixit. Nice to meet you. This is my wife, Bhavna."

Brad shook their hands. He also did a prayerful half-bow as a 'respect thing' for their foreign religion or culture or whatever.

"So, Dr. Dixit and... Mrs. Dixit—so nice to meet you! Are you new to this area?"

Brad needed to figure out their combined annual income. He was hoping the guy was the surgeon and not the other way around—female MDs made less—but you never knew with their kind... things were very ass-backwards in India or Pakistan or wherever the fuck they came from.

"We have never owned a home in this county."

"Well, you picked the perfect county! And the perfect, very upscale neighborhood! Yet, surprisingly affordable. This home is listed for only $4.5. It's 2.4 acres with the Olympic inground, the 4-car garage and nice amenities like the elevator, central air, everywhere - even in the garages — surround sound movie theater and the full house generator."

"That is nice."

After visiting the incredible kitchen and 'living spaces' on the ground floor, they traveled up the dramatic dual stairway and made their way through the second floor of the home, inspecting the six bedrooms and seven marbled baths. They were all taking a breather, peering out of the 'cascading' window wall on the second-floor landing—a dramatic 'water feature'—a great use of open space. The scene of the sloping valley to the northwest was breathtaking. But there was that odd burned-out looking structure just a quarter mile away in the distance.

"Brad, what happened over there?" Dr. Dixit was pointing to the damaged structure.

"Oh that? Yes, a neighbor's home was unfortunately struck by lightning. A crazy thing. But, FYI, this home is 'to Code,' grounded and with surge suppression throughout. All good here."

"So, do you get a lot of lightning strikes out here?"

Brad was caught off guard. He was not a fucking meteorologist.

"Well... No more than any other place in the county—I think...." He was nodding, happily. And then he regrouped. "And if an electrical storm does hit and knock down the wires or blow a transformer, this place has the standby, natural gas, electric generator. You'll never have to worry about a loss of power."

"Oh—is power loss a problem out here?"

"Well, yeah. Definitely. The electrical lines out here are all above ground and on poles. Primitive. That's why everybody has a generator. Anytime there's a storm—boom, out goes the power. I live out here, too. I've got a generator, too. It's a lifesaver. This home has one of the best! The thing is, you'll never have to worry about a power loss. As soon as power goes out, the generator immediately kicks in. You'll barely notice."

He didn't want to tell the Doctor that his own generator was a portable gasoline model. But it did work, at least.

·

Like before, the phone line rang at least a dozen times before being picked-up. There was never a voicemail option.

"Yes."

"Reg? It's Kev."

"Oh, hey Kev—hang on for just a second."

Dixit heard the same odd clicking and humming sounds as before.

"Kev, could you please confirm that you're phoning from a landline?"

"Yes, I am."

"Of course—sorry to put you through that each time." There was a pause. "Well, I've got some good news, Kev! You were right! You got three out of four hits!"

Dixit was thinking that Reg sounded positively giddy. He hadn't heard Reg sound this happy since their Ignatius days. He wasn't sure if it was due to his drug regimen or just normal human joy. He was not going to ask.

"Excellent Reg. Tell me which days and what the card was used for."

"Ok the dates are Thursday September 7, Wednesday September 13 and Thursday September 14. And like you thought, always the same restaurant for a meal and—truly unbelievable to me, like you suspected—the same show each time! 'Clonk!' at the National Theatre. That's the one where gymnasts or acrobats or whatever they are beat metal trash cans to a pulp with sticks!" Reg was almost laughing now.

"Excellent Reg. That tells me my hunch is worth pursuing."

"C'mon Kev! Don't keep me hanging! What does it mean? The man travels to DC several times within a short period—several days in a row even and eats at the same restaurant at the same

time and goes to the same horrible show that he's already seen—
three times?"

"Well, I'd rather not say until I get it nailed down. I want
to be able to give you the whole picture at once." Kev knew his
theory had promise, but he was missing some pieces.

"Aw, ok. I didn't think you would!"

• • •

Dixit was smiling. "So, may I pour you some gripe water my
beautiful?"

Bhavna took a seat next to Kev on the couch. She embraced
him gently and kissed his cheek. "Yes you may, my lotus!"

Dixit revealed the wine bottle to Bhavna, doing his best
imitation of a snooty sommelier. "Premier Cru, Dundalk Liquors,
2017." He unscrewed the cap, dramatically, and poured each a
glass of urine-yellow Chardonnay. He raised his glass for a toast.
"To more free time!"

They clinked glasses and each took a sip. Their faces involuntarily puckered.

Dixit put his glass down. "Needs time to breathe."

Bhavna placed her glass on the coffee table next to Kev's.
"Ok, I'll leave mine here overnight... so, how are you doing with
Reg's thing?" She had been concerned about all the time he had
been spending. Pretty much every second of his 'free' time. It had
been weeks now.

"Well, I'm almost there. But I'm a little stuck on a couple
things. Do we still enjoy Doctor-Patient Confidentiality?"

Bhavna rolled her eyes. "Here we go again. Of course, silly
man. 'You can give me your thoughts, freely. You may share without concern.'"

"Ok, hang on..." Kev left the room and opened the Incident

Report on his PC. He transcribed several phrases onto a sheet of note paper and returned to the couch.

"So, these are some hieroglyphs from the Fire Department's Incident Report. I'm trying to figure out what they mean. And, it's not that I'm being too lazy to ask the County Fire Department—I've been told not to under any circumstances."

The paper said: 'bad plug-tender' and '2d tender.' He handed the paper to Bhavna.

"Sounds like Elvis—'Love me Tender?'"

"'Ha ha.' So, I had thought that the 'plug' referred to maybe an electrical outlet that had a faulty plug that was plugged in. But there's nothing in the Incident Report that mentions an electrical fire cause by a faulty outlet. A 'tender' in the fire world is a kind of water tanker truck. But I can't figure out what that has to do with an electrical outlet or plug."

"What does the report say caused the fire?"

"It says lightning most likely struck the house, sending a huge electrical charge into the house's gas pipes. The house had what they call "corrugated stainless steel tubing." Apparently, this kind of piping had problems in the past and is susceptible to damage from lightning. The Report said that the gas line was probably installed back before the regulations changed. The lines now have to be 'bonded'—basically grounded—to prevent this problem. The Report said the electrical charge most likely burned through the piping, allowing the gas to leak out and pool in the basement where it was ignited. The piping was burned through and too damaged to confirm whether or not it was bonded."

"Ok, but Reg doesn't think it was lightning?"

"Well, we're looking into alternative theories. That's why I need your brain. What do the words mean to you?"

"A bad plug. I don't know about the tender thing. But besides

being an electrical plug. What about a 'fire plug'—a hydrant?"
The notion had not occurred to Dixit.

• • •

It was an odd request. A 'courtesy,' her Precinct Commander
had called it. The Captain said the City Detective wanted to
review a traffic matter that she handled about a month before.
The Detective would meet her at the coffee shop. He'd find
her because she'd be in uniform. He'd bring a copy of the police
report.

Corporal Jensen was not looking forward to wasting her
precious break time with some macho cop from the City's CID.
She had grabbed her coffee and found an open table. They'd call
her number when her egg sandwich was ready.

She carefully sipped her coffee. She saw a bunch of col-
lege-aged kids and a few 'dad' types with Ravens caps. She saw
an older Indian-looking man at the next table. This was going to
be a 'no show' because there were definitely no other cops in the
house.

She heard her number, picked up her sandwich and took her
time enjoying breakfast while reading her phone. She was about
to leave when the Indian looking man in the blue blazer walked
over.

"Officer Jensen? I am Kev Dixit—from the City?"
She did a double-take. She stood and shook his extended
hand.

"Nice to meet you Detective. Just call me 'Jen'—my
nickname."

"Of course! Please call me Kev."

As they were sitting back down, she wondered why he had
waited to introduce himself. He had been sitting a few yards away

the whole time.

"Were you waiting for me to finish my food?"

"Yes! I didn't want to invade your tranquil space."

"Well, thank you."

She was thinking 'what an odd old cop.'

"So, Jen, take a look at this one."

He handed her a copy of her police report—a traffic incident.

"Do you remember this? Basically, the driver suffered a seizure or something and was taken to the ER after he ran his car up on the sidewalk."

She took the photocopy and glanced it over.

"Yes, I do—very well."

She remembered that she got stuck working that Labor Day and was not happy about it, but she kept that part to herself.

"The old guy—I mean he was like a senior citizen—was very shaken up when we got to him. His airbag really saved him. Seemed like a nice old guy—just confused. He said he had taken a wrong turn somewhere. We had no reason to believe he was DUI or anything other than his having some sort of health incident that caused him to lose consciousness and run his car off the road."

Kev was nodding, taking it all in.

"I felt bad for him because he had just purchased that car—a used car—really ancient Ford, but then that happened. The car was totaled, of course."

She was thinking that it was probably virtually totaled at the time of purchase.

"Yes, understood. Now, when he was being helped out of the wreck, did you notice whether he was wearing eyeglasses?"

Jen's eyes lit up. She looked on, warily. "Well no. He was not wearing his glasses—but I found his glasses inside the wreck and gave them to the EMT so that he'd have them at the hospital."

"Ok—do you remember, were the glasses folded together like when they get put back in the case or open like when they're worn?"

She was thinking, 'Ok, now this is getting ridiculous.'

She smiled, broadly, and chuckled.

"Detective—are you pranking me? Seriously. Who's behind this? Sal or James? James, right? Are you even a detective—no, right? I didn't think so!"

James was the biggest clown of their Academy class.

Dixit looked on, confusedly, trying to figure it out. "Prank? No, please Officer Jen. I am absolutely serious. Why did you think this was a prank?"

"Well, c'mon. You asked about whether the glasses were folded or not — just like the other guy."

"Other guy?"

"Yes, another... man... who said he worked for the insurance company tracked me down a few weeks after the crash and asked the same thing about the glasses—folded or not. He said that, should anyone else come by and ask the same thing, take his name and number and then contact him."

She was glad she had caught herself. She almost used the word 'geezer' to describe the insurance man—this Kev guy was also ancient.

Dixit was rubbing his chin looking down at the table.

"Folded right?"

"Yes, folded."

"Ok—now, cop to cop, I need you to agree that you will not contact the insurance guy."

He quickly produced his shield and placed on the table so that she could see he was a real cop.

"Oh—don't worry, Detective. I never had any intention of contacting that civilian. But here's the guy's name and phone number if you want it."

She scrolled down her phone and held it open for Kev to see.

• • •

As before, the phone line rang at least a dozen times before being picked-up. There was never a voicemail option.

"Yes."

"Reg? It's Kev."

"Oh, hey Kev—hang on for just a second."

Kev heard the usual clicking and buzzing noises. "By the way, Reg, I'm on a land line."

Dixit figured he would alter the pattern, slightly. "Ah—ok, Kev...."

Marquis still wanted to ask Dixit about the land line but he stopped himself.

"So, Kev—have you come up with a conclusion now? You think it was arson?"

"Well, yes. I do think arson was very likely."

He took a deep breath—this was going to be tricky to explain.

"Well, what did you find?"

"Ok. I don't believe the home was struck by lightning. But the storm was directly responsible for causing the fire."

Marquis was starting to feel disappointed. This was not sounding much like arson.

"Ok?"

"Alright—so, a plumber colludes with Herman to make alterations to Herman's gas line in his basement. Picture a simple gas valve added to existing piping that, when triggered, would open to release gas—to begin leaking gas—into the home."

"Ok—what is the trigger?"

"The standby electric generator. When the generator kicks in upon a power failure, an electric relay causes the valve to open. The generator would be pulling in gas to fuel the engine but some of the gas would begin leaking inside the home."

Marquis saw the flaw, immediately. "But Kev, how could someone safely live in a home like that? If a storm hit or some other problem caused the generator to turn on, anyone inside the home could be a victim of the gas leak?"

"Ok, but remember that it is very easy to turn a generator on or off. A simple on-off switch is under the hood. Picture Herman keeping the generator off anytime he was in the house—only switching on at certain select times."

"Ok. So, the generator had to turn on. How could he be away from the house and still turn on the generator? They can be set to turn on by a timer, right? They have a self-testing thing, right? That's what he did?"

'Here comes the crazy part,' Kev thought. "Well, no. The fire investigator checked the generator thoroughly. Its weekly self-test was set for Saturday mornings at 10:00 AM. Herman could not have set the timer to engage on the evening of Wednesday the 20th because he, or someone, would have then had to switch it back before the fire investigator had checked it out. That simply did not happen. For what it's worth, the generator was running just fine when the Fire Department arrived. The Incident Report tells us that they switched it off. And the utility company had to be called in to shut down the gas—they wound up shutting down the main for the whole subdivision as a precaution."

"Ok. So…?"

"Ok, here's how he did it. Suppose you check out the weather forecast—maybe the 5 day. Suppose there's a date where there's a great probability of bad weather—almost a certainty of a storm. Remember, the fire occurred in late summer. Late afternoon and evening thunderstorms hit all the time in this region. And, I understand that downed lines and power failures during storms are commonplace in that area. Now, pick a date where the meteorological conditions are ripe for a late afternoon or evening storm."

"Yes."

"Now, Herman needs to engage the generator so that it will function on that date. But, he also needs to be away from the home and establish an alibi. He can't be seen near the home that night—nor does he want to be trapped in his own fire. So, he books a restaurant and a show in DC. He can travel there in less than two hours. In fact, his credit card record confirmed he was away at the restaurant and attended a show on the night of the fire."

"Ok. And you asked me about those earlier dates because you had checked meteorological records just before the date of the fire. Because that's what Herman did?"

"Correct. Herman never knew for sure whether there would be a power failure caused by a storm on any given date. But he knew that such happened all the time in his neighborhood. The odds were in his favor. He just needed to be patient. He checked the weather and on the night of Thursday September 7, he left town and created the credit card record. But that night was a dud. The power to his home did not go out. So, he tried again on the nights of Wednesday the 13th and Thursday the 14th. Two more duds. There might have been storms on those nights, but none of the storms knocked the power out at his home. But on the night of Wednesday the 20th, he headed back down to DC just as before. His plan worked. Power was knocked out in the neighborhood and the generator turned on, which triggered the opening of the gas valve inside the house."

Marquis found another flaw. "But if lightning didn't strike the home, what sparked the gas explosion?"

"Almost certainly his lighting system. Herman had his lighting on a master timer. Lights throughout the home could be engaged at specified times throughout the day and night. The simple electrical contact of a switch engaging a light would be enough to ignite a gas leak. Picture Herman setting the lighting to engage and disengage at various time through the night, which could happen, thanks to the generator which kept electric power going following the power failure."

There was silence.

"Reg?"

"Yeah, Kev—just taking it in..."

Kev added: "But there was another problem I had to work through."

"Another problem?"

"Well, you saw the Fire Incident Report. The Fire Department got to the home within eight minutes of the fire being called-in by the neighbor. That's pretty fast. The fire was then immediately upgraded to a 'two alarm' and the second group of trucks arrived 8 minutes or so after that."

"Ok?"

"Well, the house was almost 8,000 square feet. Even with the fire and a gas explosion, it should not have been a total loss. The Fire Department got there quickly. The fire should have been extinguished sooner. A substantial portion of the home should have been saved."

"Why wasn't it?"

"Water. The engines carry a lot of water but they needed to hook up to a hydrant for this blaze. But there was no nearby hydrant."

"Why not?"

"Because Herman had paid someone to run the hydrant over a couple weeks before. That meant that the Fire crew had to call for a water tanker truck, which took 10 more minutes to arrive. And then they had to order-up a second tanker truck, which likewise came 10 minutes after that. All the while, the fire was staying alive and spreading. Ultimately, the house was declared a total loss, securing the maximum insurance payout."

Again, there was silence.

"How do you know that Herman orchestrated all this?"

"Well, it took me a while to figure out that the local hydrant had been destroyed. When I took a drive through the neighborhood, I saw a hydrant there, just a few doors down from Herman's home. I thought nothing of it at the time. But the notes in the Incident Report indicated a 'bad plug,' meaning the hydrant wasn't functioning. And the Report indicated calling-up the tankers for more water. I checked with the County and saw that there had been a standing work order to replace the hydrant at the time of the fire. The work order indicated that the old hydrant had been run over by a car and the water line sealed off. The hydrant was eventually replaced, but after the fire."

He didn't want to tell Reg that Bhavna had helped him figure out the hydrant thing. Reg might not understand their confidentiality arrangement.

"Ok, but what makes you think Herman was behind having it destroyed?"

"Well, I got a copy of the Police Report on the traffic incident relating to the hydrant. As I suspected, the car that ran over the hydrant was wrecked and the driver injured. The car was an old beater, recently purchased. The driver's name is Daniel Platt. I— very discretely—made an inquiry of the County traffic cop who arrived at the scene and helped EMS get Platt to the hospital. I know you said not to contact the County cops about the fire— and I didn't. I contacted them strictly about the auto accident— not the fire."

Dixit was hoping that his contacting the County cops would not piss Reg off—or at least not too much.

"Sure Kev—sounds ok. But what makes you think the Platt guy deliberately ran his car over the hydrant? Did the traffic cop think so?"

"No—at least I doubt it. I saw from the Traffic Incident Report that the guy had a restricted license—he had to wear contacts or glasses. I simply asked the County cop if she found his glasses in the wreck and whether they were folded."

There was more silence.

"Platt's prescription glasses were found in the car. If the incident had been a true accident, Platt would have been wearing his glasses when the air bag was released. The glasses would likely have been bent up and mangled by the impact of the bag on his face. Or, if they were knocked off Platt's face they would have fallen away in the open position. But if the 'accident' was delib- erate, Platt likely might have first removed his glasses and folded them and maybe placed them on the passenger seat to prevent them from being bent up by the certain impact of the air bag. The County cop found them folded and on the passenger side floor."

Kev had decided to not share the info about the insurance guy who had been checking out the same thing. 'No harm, no foul,' there.

There was more silence.

"Oh—and the last thing was that I checked online and found that Platt's son is a licensed plumber. I suspect that both father and son were paid to help Herman with his scheme. I was thinking that if the County cops brought the father in and threatened charging them both, Platt might roll to save his son. Or, vice versa, bring in the son. Then, with one of the Platts' witness statements, the County cops could charge Herman with the arson, conspiracy, etc."

There was a pause.

Dixit continued, "and, I mean, the icing on the cake would be the various times that Herman travelled to DC to wait for a storm to hit. What rational person would go see the same performance of "Clonk!" four times? It was probably the only show in town with plenty of seating available and easy to book on an instant's notice."

Dixit was thinking that no rational person would want to experience "Clonk!" even once—but he kept that to himself.

There were a few more seconds of awkward silence and then Marquis spoke, enthusiastically.

"Kev—you did it! Thank you, man! You figured it out."

"Well, you're welcome, Reg! I hope this gets you where you need to be?"

"Absolutely, Kev! Absolutely! I can't thank you, enough!"

Dixit was thinking that he was glad to help and would just keep an eye out in the newspaper for an arrest. And, once the whole thing blew over—whenever that would be—he might just contact that insurance guy. He really wanted to meet him...

"You're welcome, Reg! Don't be a stranger!"

Marquis clicked off and re-set his phone system. He sighed to himself, despondently. No one would ever believe anything so farfetched. Yes, he knew it was all very likely true. But the crime was just too crazy, too unusual for any Police Department to take seriously. He certainly would not bother his local contact in the County government about it. He would be laughed at.

He sighed, again, and walked into his kitchen. He opened the fridge and saw the can of Hawaiian Punch.

•••

Now.

Where were his clean clothes? He had just done laundry, yesterday or the day before. And clean underwear. He looked around groggily. What the hell time was it? He gazed down and saw a piece of lint or cereal in his beard. He picked it out and stared at it. Probably puffed wheat. It made him hungry for a bowl, so he bent down to his miniature refrigerator looking for milk. But there was no milk. Other unpleasant things came into view, so he shut the door, quickly. He would defrost it, too, later. He meant to, before. There was time. There was no rush. He could use a shot of booze.

He walked around in his underpants—one of his two pairs—indelibly stained. He trawled over piles of clothing heaped upon his furniture: a massive, industrial wooden spool used as a table, a 1990's era futon, some pieces missing, and several large cardboard boxes that once held something. He went from pile to pile and sniffed at the clothing. Wow. And he had just done the laundry. He seemed to have no wearable clothes. And then he happened upon his biohazardous waste reclamation suit, a bright orange jumpsuit. He pulled his filthy underpants off and placed them carefully on the heap found on top of the refrigerator. He had gained a little weight while underemployed but he squeezed into the orange jumpsuit. The crotch was not terribly comfortable against his testicles. He rubbed them. He was thinking they hadn't been used in a while. Oh well.

He left the apartment and walked along the road, barefoot. He was instinctively drawn to the Wine Shop, caddy corner, across the street. He didn't care for wine, but they carried the usual variety of booze. Then he remembered the last time he went in there with no money. Fuck. They nearly called the cops. He hadn't even caused any problems. Sometimes life was not fair.

Then he remembered the barber shop about a block away and the nice young woman at the front desk. What was her name... Julianna, Jill? She would chat for a little while and hand him a fiver from the cash drawer. He remembered now. That's what he did last time. He went and got the fiver, first, and then they treated him like a normal customer at the Wine Shop.

He entered the hair shop. Something was truly fucked up. His girl was sitting in her reception chair crying. Her eyes were red. A lot of the other customers were crying, screaming, wandering around. He looked over and saw a man lying on the floor. The windows had been shot to pieces—he hadn't noticed when he first walked in. There was a breeze, now.

They saw the orange tech jumpsuit. Several voices screeched. "Are you from 9-1-1? He's dead! They shot him!"

He walked over to the man on the floor. Blood was everywhere, pooling next to his body.

A woman's voice said, "I checked for a pulse and couldn't find one!"

He got down on his knees and bent over the body.

"Quick, bring me a bunch of clean towels. We have to staunch the blood flow."

Another woman's voice said, "I think he's dead!"

Towels were quickly shoved in his direction.

"You can't tell. He might be in shock. Let's get these wounds covered so I can do CPR."

He looked up at one of the faces with the towels. "Here, hold these tight against him—like this." He jammed the towels against the man's chest and stomach. The woman took over. "No—I mean really tight."

He jammed her hands with the towels into the prone body. She cringed but followed his instruction.

"That's it."

He moved closer to the man's face and looked into his eyes. Not glassy yet. Good. And then he looked more closely at the face and thought to himself, 'Christ—I think I know this guy.'

He yelled up to the crowd that had gathered, "Hey—call 9-1-1 again, man! This is the City. You gotta call more than once!"

He opened the man's mouth with his hands and breathed air into the man's lungs. He put his hands over the woman's holding the towels and began gently pushing against the man's ribcage— but not too fiercely because of the wounds.

And then he heard the sirens, first from a distance and then quickly approaching.

• • •

Three Days from Now

It was nice being back home, again. His parents were probably out, but they wouldn't mind his visiting. He was looking for his Tony Award. He knew it had to be in the home, somewhere, because his parents would have certainly been displaying the award. He wandered around the living room glancing up at the book shelves. They looked a little different than he remembered. He checked through the lower shelves looking to see if the Tony was hidden behind some books.

It was odd that the layout of the home was not exactly as he remembered it. The dining room was back behind the kitchen—so that must have been changed somehow. He looked around on the buffet in the dining room, but saw only a few framed photos of his mom and dad. He was kind of missing them and really wished they had been home for his visit.

He went to the corner china cabinet and kept looking. It wasn't there. He knew his parents must have been displaying it, somewhere.

He wandered down the hallway to his old bedroom. It seemed to be on the wrong side of the hall, but it was definitely his room. He looked in to see his goldfish bowl. He was glad to see Pup and Snazzy swimming happily. He hadn't seen them in a long time! Pup was still chubbier than Snazzy.

He was thirsty. He would go to the kitchen to get a little water for himself and a glassful to top-off the level of the bowl.

And then it occurred to him—he would not have won his Tony, yet. This was his home when he was a kid. The Tony wouldn't be there, yet. He would have to come back later, at a point when he will have won the award. Maybe he'd see his folks then.

He was hearing something in the background. From down the hall? He heard his name...

"Waxley, c'mon guy—wake up. We didn't come all the way down here to watch you snooze! C'mon Chris—yoo hoo!"

He looked over to his companion.

"Can you believe he's snoring—in front of guests?"

She shook her head, "I can't believe he's alive! I think we should let him sleep... that's what the doctors would want, right?"

The Troll moved closer to Waxley's side. "Jesus—so that's his face without a clean shave? I don't think I've seen him with stubble...He's a hot mess. Hey Waxley—c'mon, wake up, Amigo!"

Waxley saw his old bedroom evaporate before his eyes and realized he was in pain. But he was also very groggy and very thirsty. He squinted and the face of Golding came into focus.

"Hey Chris, welcome back? Did ya have a nice snooze?" The Troll was smiling, broadly.

"Wha?"

He was so damn thirsty, but there was no cup of water on the bed table. He could barely move his head—it was all so foggy. And then the bad news hit home: he had never won a Tony. Why did he think he had won a Tony?

He blinked and saw the other person. He had seen her before. Yes. They had all danced together—the Hokey Pokey... What was her name?

"So Waxley—congratulations, you're a Jew!"

"What—Troll?"

"Yeah, it's the only way I could get us up here to see you in the ICU. I had the desk change your religious affiliation from Catholic to Jewish so that they would let me, the "Rabbi" and Ruthann, the "Shomer" up here to attend to your religious needs! Pretty good, huh?"

Ruthann whispered, "I don't think he would know what a shomer is, Golding. Don't tell him!"

Chris mumbled, "can you get me some water, Troll?" His voice sounded like crushed gravel.

"Hey—sorry Amigo. They said no fluids. I think it's because you're so full of holes that the water would leak right out of you!" Troll was smiling broadly again.

"Stop, that Golding! Don't be such an ass!" Ruthann was standing, arms folded, trying not to smile.

"No, Chris—they said outside they have to monitor your

fluid intake and shit. So, we don't want to screw anything up, now that you decided to live."

Ruthann shook her head in disgust.

Waxley was starting to come out of it.

He croaked: "I was dreaming about being home—when I was a kid. Thinking about my mom and dad, I guess..."

His throat was scratchy and it was hard to talk.

"Your mom and dad? You know Waxley, the Rabbi Joseph Telushkin once remarked, and I quote: 'even from earliest times, Judaism promoted the parent-child relationship.' But one of his students questioned the Rabbi, saying, 'but, Rabbi, isn't it true that the first commandment God gave to Abraham was for Abraham to leave his father's home?' The Rabbi said, 'yes, but he was 75 at the time; he was entitled.'"

Waxley began laughing... a frightening, croaking sound.

"Jesus. He sounds worse than you with that sinus thing, Golding!"

Waxley made a 'stop' motion with his hands. Laughing was downright painful.

"Ok, ok. I'll quit with the jokes!"

An ICU nurse heard the ruckus and entered the room. "Folks, this guy needs to take it easy in here." She lifted his head gently to readjust it on the pillow.

"We have to take care of our VIPs!"

"Water?"

She checked the clock. Close enough. "Hang on."

She left the room and quickly returned with a small clear plastic cup of ice water with a straw. One ounce.

He reached out gratefully for the cup and began to drink.

"Hey, go easy there, Batman—sip, don't gulp."

He nodded, 'ok.' He felt better. He put the cup back on his

bed table.

He looked over at the Troll and Ruthann with a puzzled look. "So—you two?"

Troll was shaking his head, 'no,' vehemently. "No, Waxley—we can't stand each other, but we have, like, a... 'truce?'"

Troll looked over to Ruthann for affirmation. Ruthann shook her head in agreement. "Yes, my parents were hellbent to marry me off to this lard ass and I told them in no uncertain terms to forget it! I said to my mother, 'seriously, Mom? Golding? This man who works at a funeral home? You want that for me? You know, what a treat, coming home to a fat, boring mortician every day? Laugh a minute. No way!'"

Golding was nodding along, earnestly.

"So, you know they dragged me to that wedding a few weeks back and of course, I tried to avoid Golding at all costs. I see he shows up with a guy 'friend' as a date—Ha! Whatever.... But then, I could not believe my eyes, Chris, when you dragged this fat tub of lard out onto the dance floor! I never laughed so much in my life!"

Golding nodded, proudly.

"Where had you guys figured out those hilarious dance routines? That whole bit from 'Footloose?' And I had not seen that stupid 'Humpty Dance' since MTV had videos! And you both knew the words, too!"

She began laughing, almost hysterically, but quickly lowered the volume when a tech came into the room to remove Waxley's finished cup of water.

"So, then when you both got up to do the Hokey Pokey—well I laughed my ass off and had to join in!"

Golding added, "so, Chris, it was great 'cause Ruthann disliked the idea of being stuck with me, just as much as I could not stand the idea of being stuck with her! We had that in common! So, we hang out sometimes. That's it."

Chris was taking it all in, understanding it, somewhat. He nodded.

• • •

She had been receiving texts from her old girlfriends all through the night, but didn't see them until the next morning, due to the time difference. She and Worth would be flying out from Vienna to Milan in just a few hours. She couldn't believe what she was reading. Her old 'ex' was shot to pieces in some nasty place in the City and was barely kept alive in Intensive Care? She was horrified at the violence but damned glad he had survived! She began to feel sad for Chris and wondered just how low he had sunk to wind-up like that? She had always warned him about getting a real job—anything but acting—and this was just the kind of thing she feared. Shot-up in Baltimore, a victim of some kind of street violence. A statistic. What the hell had he been up to in the City? But, thank God, at least he was alive.

She sighed to herself. She knew their breakup, years ago, was the right thing. Chris would not have made the kind of husband and father that Worth had. Things were really perfect, now. The kids were away at school and she and Worth could finally take that dream vacation.

Her father was right about Chris. And, it was kind of lucky that Dad's old school friend had told him about his new hire—about how impressed he was with 'Jefferson Davis Worthington,' a true Southern gentleman. Worth had been coxswain for his crew at the University—a champion—with several regatta cups to prove it. His parents and family were well regarded, socially, and politically prominent. Worth had good hobbies and interests. He loved being a Civil War Reenactor.

And she was proud when Worth set-up his own financial consulting company, "Power 10." Yes, the economy had been 'up and down' but Worth was going to pull-in a good salary, soon. Start-ups were always difficult. Meeting the right clients was the key. His travel away from home would definitely pay off! Once he got the right client mix, he'd be back home a lot more. In the meantime, she was more than happy to continue working. She loved her work. And, with her salary able to pay for the nanny, she knew they were not missing a beat as a family!

And now, they could finally relax together and enjoy their vacation. She relished their four-day stay in the heart of Vienna—the museums, the Opera House. And wonderful food! And it was ok that Worth could hang back at the hotel and sleep-in those days. He needed the rest. His job was stressful.

Next, her ultimate dream—on to Fashion Week 2020, in Milan!

• • •

Dixit saw the attending physician juggling his time among four units. He figured he could flash his badge and get in to see Waxley.

"So, Doctor—Detective Dixit. How's Chris doing?"

Doctor Risman looked over at Dixit's badge and ID. "Pretty well, Detective. He's stable and the first set of surgeries are all done and appear to all be holding, ok. We need to get him stable for the next set. He took an incredible amount of shot to his body. I've never seen anything like it. You're a policeman, so you know what that stuff does to the body—to tissue. It destroys organs—but, thankfully, organ damage was minimal. Very lucky, in that. There's going to be a lot of scarring though. But he's made

it so far. I think he can get through the rest. He's one tough...
guy."

He was going to say "motherfucker," but didn't want to seem
crude. He was not a field surgeon, anymore. These were almost all
civilians. He kept having to remember.

"That's great, Doctor. Any idea when they'll cut him loose
from ICU?"

"Hard to say. But I'd guess, in three or four days. We'll need
to get him off of a lot of this." He was pointing to the network of
tubes and bottles hanging from the IV stand. "But he'll get there."

"How's the kid?" Dixit was hoping for at least as good news.

"Well—not good Detective. Not good. He's on life support.
He's still alive, but I can't say for how long. He's just down there if
you want to stop in. Nobody's in there. Nobody's been in there."
He pointed towards a unit a couple door's down.

"Ok. Thanks Doctor."

And with that, Risman quickly moved on to the next unit.

Dixit rapped on the outside of the unit door frame. "Hey
Chris! How are you feeling?" He hadn't noticed that Waxley had
a visitor.

"Hey Kev!" Clay Switzer got up, slowly, from the chair. He
limped over to shake hands.

Dixit saw that Switzer was in fatigues. Yet, he knew he had
been mustered out on medical following the I.E.D. incident just
outside the Green Zone.

"Hey—Clay? Wow, good to see you, man!" He thought that
the facial scarring had improved quite a bit since last time.

"Kev, see?" Switzer was pointing down to his fatigues. "I figured if I dressed in my fatigues, they'd let me in here. It worked!"

Dixit smiled but looked puzzled.

"Oh, this is for C.A.P.—Civil Air Patrol. I'm still a civilian.

It feels good to be useful! C.A.P.'s a good thing. I've made tons of friends. But, there's some really incredible news that no one in media has picked-up on, yet. So, listen to this—even though I'm legally blind and deaf in my right eye and right ear, I applied to Spacex. I told them that I can still fly better than most of their fully functional pilots and knew I could make it into space. So, Elon... Mr. Musk, heard about it and said he was going to help me! The guy is paying for my cochlear implant and experimental surgery to implant a microelectrode array into my visual cortex—yes! The guy is paying for brain surgery for me—all out of his own pocket—so that I might see out of that eye again! Unbelievable! And, I will get to space!"

"Wow, Clay! Congratulations—that is some of the best news I have heard...maybe ever? Except maybe for this guy, who somehow survived two rounds of buckshot, point blank...".

At that, Waxley began to rouse himself. "What? What did you say?" His grumbling sound was about two octaves lower than what they were used to. He sounded something like Johnny Cash on steroids, but with a bad throat infection.

"Oh hey, Chris—it's Kev and Clay! How are you doing, my man?"

He rasped: "I'm good, Kev! All good! Maybe a little groggy..."

"That's ok, Chris. Don't strain yourself. We just wanted to check in with you to see how you're feeling!"

"Ok!"

"So, listen, Chris—Deputy Commissioner Luchowski is supposed to drop by to see how you're doing. That's kind of a big deal!"

"Oh—cool, Kev." Waxley nodded and drifted back off to sleep.

Dixit looked over to Switzer. "You know, your brother saved his life."

"Yeah! I know! I am so proud of that asshole! I will be in attendance when they give him a medal, or the key to the City or whatever the fuck they do down in this place."

"Yeah, yeah—me too, Clay!"

Dixit didn't have the heart to tell him that his brother had been arrested for disturbing the peace during the incident and was now temporarily residing in a halfway house on Eager Street. And he didn't look forward to telling Waxley that the guy who shot him was apprehended just a few minutes later and couple miles down the road. But the guy would not give up. And that the guy got the worst of a shootout with a Patrol Officer. The 'guy' was a 15-year-old boy. He would drop in on the kid before he left.

Dixit thought he heard a familiar voice speaking with the doctor outside the unit. He left Switzer with Waxley.

He waited for the two to finish up.

"Hey—Deputy Commissioner! Thanks for stopping by, here."

"Hey, Kev, good to see you! It's been a while!" They embraced warmly.

"How's Michael and the kids?"

"Doing well, Kev, really well! His are all married-off and ours is a junior in college, but all good. How's Bhavna and your... two kids?"

"Yep, just the two. The oldest—my son, Vadin—he's in grad school, if you can believe it. And Beth, our youngest, is a senior in high school. And Bhavna's great! We're all good!"

"That's great, Kev!"

She pointed over to the room. "The surgeon said our guy is going to be ok."

"Yeah—it's a miracle."

She peeked into the room to see that both Waxley and Switzer had nodded off. She dropped her voice. "So, I've spent the last 48 hours talking the Commissioner off the ledge. Can you believe he wanted to charge your guy with impersonating a police officer?"

"What? You can't be serious."

"No—I'm serious. It's part of his 'anti-vigilante' thing. Absolutely unbelievable. The media are making your pal a hero and that dimwit wants to have him arrested. So, I said, 'Mr. Commissioner—you know the optics might not be right for that? This guy was not impersonating the Police—he was defending himself, and others, by using non-violent measures. He was using the only means of self-defense he had—his acting abilities. We should consider adopting a spi— I mean, a 'narrative' on how a local born and bred Baltimore actor risked his own life to save the lives of everyone in that hair salon.' I told him, 'It's a tribute to the genius and talent of our local arts community. And the bravery of a good man.' And, thank God, he's going to go with that!"

"Way to go Melody! Phew! Nice work!"

He was thinking, 'yeah,' his protégé was going to make a damn good Commissioner one day—hopefully soon.

"He's still worried about the boy. We're all praying that he makes it because this is a bad time for a kid to die at the hands of a cop around here—you know?"

"Yeah. I hear you. They told me he was hanging in there but...."

"Yeah, that's what the surgeon was telling me."

They stood quietly for a moment.

"Oh, Kev—I almost forgot. I didn't have a chance to thank you in person for helping Michael's brother. The guy in Aviation told Todd that your moral support was very helpful as he completed the investigation and made the arrest."

"Oh, of course! You bet."

"Ok, Kev. I've got to get out in front of media in about 40 minutes—so tell your guy he's going to be the most popular actor in Maryland before he wakes up. Maybe in America. I mean, seriously—it's going to be batshit for this guy. His dance card is going to get punched every which way of Sunday—hope he's up to it?"

"Waxley? Oh hell, yeah!"

The two shook hands.

"Thanks Melody—thanks for everything...."

• • •

Later that evening, Waxley was gently jostled awake.

"Wha?"

"Hi Chris. I'm Doctor Eberhardt, your chief surgeon. How are you feeling?"

He rasped, "oh, hi Doctor. I feel pretty good. But I'm like really sore around the waist. And my leg, too."

"Understandable. We had to perform several surgeries and remove a lot of pellet fragments."

He wanted to tell him he was lucky to be alive and that if it weren't for the good luck of that physician coming along, just at the right time, he'd not be here, but he figured he'd learn all about that from others. He'd let him get back to sleep.

He finished his examination and marked up his chart.

He sighed. Quiet had finally come over the busy ward. He stood by the doorway and took a break, checking his phone. The news out of CDC was not good. Not good at all. A storm was brewing. He wondered what his ICU would look like in a month's time? It worried him, deeply. His old classmate in CDC had phoned him to say, 'David, if you read anything optimistic in the press—forget it. It's bullshit. This is going to be bad. Really, really bad.'

He sighed again to himself. He was reading some more about Wuhan and what was going on in northern Italy. He thought he heard a sandpaper sound and realized his patient was trying to speak to him.

"... will I?"

"I'm sorry Chris—did you say something? I didn't catch what you were saying?"

"I said: when this is all done, will I be able to sing again?"

Eberhardt thought about the mild scarring of his vocal cords—he knew that would all heal with time.

"Yes. You'll sing even better than before, Chris. Better." Eberhardt went back to his phone.

Waxley took a deep breath and sighed. "Thanks Doc...."

He laid his head back onto his pillow and rested peacefully.

About the Author

J. P. (Paul) Rieger is a real estate attorney and amateur musician who grew up in Baltimore and now resides in Towson. *Clonk!* is Paul's second work of fiction following his 2013 publication of *The Case Files of Roderick Misely, Consultant.* He greatly enjoys music, books and humor. He is old, but has retained most of his teeth and hair.

Apprentice House Press

Loyola University Maryland

Apprentice House is the country's only campus-based, student-staffed book publishing company. Directed by professors and industry professionals, it is a nonprofit activity of the Communication Department at Loyola University Maryland.

Using state-of-the-art technology and an experiential learning model of education, Apprentice House publishes books in untraditional ways. This dual responsibility as publishers and educators creates an unprecedented collaborative environment among faculty and students, while teaching tomorrow's editors, designers, and marketers.

Eclectic and provocative, Apprentice House titles intend to entertain as well as spark dialogue on a variety of topics. Financial contributions to sustain the press's work are welcomed. Contributions are tax deductible to the fullest extent allowed by the IRS.

To learn more about Apprentice House books or to obtain submission guidelines, please visit www.apprenticehouse.com.

Apprentice House
Communication Department
Loyola University Maryland
4501 N. Charles Street
Baltimore, MD 21210
410-617-5265
info@apprenticehouse.com
www.apprenticehouse.com